SEA OF SHADOW

SARAH K. L. WILSON

ALSO BY SARAH K. L. WILSON

Find all of Sarah's books at:

www.sarahklwilson.com

———

Bluebeard's Secret Series

Seven Swords Series

Fae Hunter Series

Bridge of Legends Series

Phoenix Heart Series

Dragon School

Married by War

CHAPTER ONE

"You are whole as long as you have your shadow," Stekkan repeats slowly, hands trembling despite an overwhelmingly calm expression as he looks from me to Vargaard, and back again. He's seeing my shadow guardian for the second time. I try to catch my breath as I look around us at the rustling grass and the loose dirt of the shepherd's trail, the darkness of velvet night, and the bright moon highlighting fluffy clouds. It looks too pastoral to be within walking distance of the burning hell behind us. I steal a single glance backward and wish I had not. We are on the top of a hill —
before us, grassy farm fields and towns. Behind us, burning, screaming, and pillars of fire-tinted smoke.

On Stekkan's shoulder, his spirit macaw whispers, "*Mercy.*"

Stekkan carefully sets the Mercy Blade in my hands and I grip it tightly, grateful when it dulls the pain in my shoulder and leg. I'm gasping from being brought back to this physical world, sinking into the relief of no longer being battered by spirits as Vargaard carries me, but also wrung and squeezed with pain from my wounds.

Vargaard is strangely silent, seeming almost frozen as he stares at Stekkan, and something in my throat feels tight as I realize that he's not my secret alone any longer. Sudden fear and defensiveness claw through me.

"*Calm.*" It's all he says to me, and it is somehow worse, as he looks at Stekkan and not at me. His expression is hard and cold as stone, as if he is weighing and judging the duke and the tiniest fraction leaning to the wrong side will spell both our dooms.

"How long has he been there?" Stekkan isn't holding the Tranquility Sword. It's nestled in the grass beside him as if he were afraid to put it in his belt. I understand that fear. I do not like to let go of my blade, either.

"Since before I met you." My voice is rough with the dryness in my throat. "How did you bring me here?"

I look to Vargaard who looks quickly away. He will not meet my eye.

"The Tranquility Sword," Stekkan says, running a trembling hand over his face. His brown skin is pale, his brow sweaty, and more than just from physical exertion, I think. "She speaks to me — softly. She told me I could tuck you away physically in the stone that held your soul when Jendaya buried you. I wouldn't have thought of that. I guess since I did it before, I can do it again."

"Perhaps it's best saved for dire circumstances," I say, unsettled by this power he holds over me.

"*And somehow the Nakuraki made him invisible.*" Vargaard's words snap in my mind like a whip, but still, he will not turn to me. All of his attention is on my new king. I do not like this feeling worming through me. It feels like loss and broken shards. Why will he not look at me?

"I wonder why Jendaya's Nakuraki didn't mention it," Stekkan says, clutching his medallion in one fist like he's trying to hold it together.

"Perhaps because she wouldn't care." I don't have the same fascination with our enemy that he does, but then again, I'm not married to her. I don't like thinking about how he was forced into that — even if it makes him the king of our land. "She is no friend to me, after all, and probably preferred me dead."

"Perhaps." Stekkan sounds uncertain, but his eyes are still on Vargaard. "Can he speak? Is he ... is he the one who spoke to me through my travails when I carried the Mercy Sword for you? Is he like ... her?"

"Her?"

"The one in the Tranquility Sword. The white lady."

"*Of course, I speak.*" I expected exasperation or mocking from Vargaard. Instead, he sounds ... subdued. And it makes the worming, gnawing feeling worse.

I can't quite catch a breath. I can't quite ...

"*Breathe!*" Vargaard's words snap out now, whip hard.

I swallow down this terrible sick sensation and fight for even breaths.

"He seems to speak to you, and I see his shadow lips flicker, but I hear no sound any longer," Stekkan says, watching us in amazement, as if this is the most urgent thing to deal with and not the pair of us shivering in the darkness — me wounded and him soot-stained and splashed with blood not his own. "Did he ... in the tower, I thought I saw him kiss you."

Vargaard's words rumble quickly into my mind. "*I owe you a great debt, Stekkan, King of Cragspear, for carrying my Vali to safety despite great difficulty and many trials.*"

My face is on fire. I look away from Stekkan, unable to acknowledge the kiss he saw us steal.

"He says he is thankful to you for bearing me to safety and he owes you a debt," I tell him, and with my words comes the realization that this clawing, grasping feeling in my heart is jealousy. I would like to keep Vargaard all to myself. To share him even this much feels like losing something. And how selfish is that?

Vargaard's gaze whips to mine. "*If that feeling is wrong, then I am ten times wrong for I feel it every time you speak to the du— king. I feel it every time he can save you when I cannot. He may have you entirely, and I never can. He may love you as a man loves a woman and I never will and it stings me to the core.*"

We hold each other's gaze for a long moment. We are one in understanding, one in this shared vice.

"I see you looking at each other," Stekkan says and he's reverting back to himself, the strange calm washing away, and a kind of petulant frustration edging his words. "And I hope that what you're discussing is how we're going to kill my wife and stop this madness, but I have a terrible feeling that what I'm seeing on your faces isn't practical planning but something akin to romance. Is he going to kiss you again?"

I feel my face grow hot and I rip my gaze from

Vargaard's anguished intensity and to Stekkan's miserable certainty.

"It's hypocritical for you to judge who I kiss, Stekkan. I watched you throw your whole soul into kissing our mortal enemy."

Stekkan hangs his head a little. "She tastes like coconut puffs."

"I didn't need to know that," I say, my mouth twisting a little.

"A thousand ages could pass and still we would not need to know that."

Stekkan looks up, jaw set. "This explains why you rejected my marriage proposal again and again."

"Yes," I say drily, "the only explanation for any woman rejecting you is that she's in love with a spirit trapped in an ancient sword."

He nods, running a hand through his rumpled hair. "Exactly my thoughts."

I clear my throat. I don't know what to say to Stekkan and I don't know what to say to Vargaard.

"Say what you must, Vali," Vargaard says, looking solemnly out toward the horizon.

"I want to thank you, Stekkan Falrune, Duke of Catterail, King of Cragspear," I say awkwardly. "For saving my life and getting us free of the city."

He blows out a long breath. "I should say the mannerly thing — that it is my pleasure or that it was nothing. But it was not either of those things. It was not pleasant at all, and it took everything out of me and, Merciful Sovereign, I do not wish to be embraced by the lady again for a very long time."

He looks dolefully at the sword. Bitterness is laced through his expression, gilding the edges of his frown.

"Mercy. See how the mighty have fallen," his spirit macaw whispers. Stekkan reaches up and caresses her - or at least attempts it.

I swallow. I don't know what to say to that, either, but I've said my piece so I turn in my mind to Vargaard.

I owe him an apology, too.

His gaze shoots back to mine. "*No, you do not.*"

But I do. His denial of it feels like a shard in my chest. Did he ... did he not want to save me? Is that why he won't accept gratitude?

His anger and confusion are both present when he stares intently at me. "*Have I ever wanted anything else except to save you?*"

I saw, I tell him. Somehow I saw you while you were in there. The Fisher King had you. He was drawing you up. You could have gone to the happiness beyond, but you did not.

He opens his shadowed lips, his face flickering so quickly from one young Vargaard to the next, head dress replaced by crown, replaced by helm, replaced by laurels — and then he's gone in a puff of black smoke and I gasp.

Gone.

I swallow, feeling miserable. He gave up too much for me. He surely must regret it, even as I do. I steal a sidelong glance at Stekkan who I catch stealing a sidelong glance at me.

He coughs uneasily and tries a grin that I think he thinks is charming. It looks like a child thanking an elder for a gift they did not want.

"Can you move?" he asks me, biting his pretty lip. "Only, we both need to keep going. And I cannot carry you."

I clutch the Mercy Sword as he helps me stand. My shoulder is painful and my left arm does not want to move. Stekkan examines it and tells me that with a cleaning and stitching he thinks it will heal. It's the leg that worries us both. It won't take my weight. Stekkan thinks it's not broken, but neither of us knows for sure. It's certainly swollen and black with bruises.

In the end, he slings an arm under my right shoulder and we both slide our swords into scabbards. He avoids his as much as possible. I cling to the hilt of mine as if it is salvation. Perhaps it is.

"Did he tell you what we should do next, before he disappeared?" Stekkan asks after maybe an hour of us hobbling out across a grassy plain. Homes dot the hills and sheep graze but we avoid them all, clinging to the trees and shadows.

I feel a pang of fear at the thought of my shadow guardian. I want to call him back. But what if he went back to the Fisher King? What if he asked for a second chance for peace? I could call and he would not return. Or, I could call and he would wish he had not returned.

And I'm not quite certain I can bear either of those things.

"We know where all the swords are now," I say a bit

huskily, trying to distract myself from my spiraling thoughts.

"For all the good it does us," Stekkan says.

"We know where Jendaya is."

"Yes, spreading her troops out across the landscape to every nation of the continent in order to subdue them with her monsters." I hear the misery in his voice. He married her to save Ghregoiren. Who knows what else he allowed done to him for the sake of that land? And now he will lose it. "We cannot prevent the spread of this. It will go everywhere, now. No one will be immune. We have no ideas on how to stop it, unless they are in this book. And we have no allies."

"We'll check the book the moment we stop to rest," I say, and realize we're already both breathless.

"I thought perhaps one of the towers. The ones the monks tend?" He shoots me a look I can't read. "We're nearly to the one I was aiming for."

He points toward a building in the darkness. It's close by horseback or even if I were well and still on foot. He must have covered a lot of ground before he drew me from the pendant again. In my present state, however, it felt like it would take far too long.

"Perhaps you should go ahead without me. There might be horses," I say. "You could bring one and that would make things faster."

He looks torn, but eventually, he nods, helping me sit under a tree and setting the heavy book beside me.

"It's a good plan," he agrees, but his face is rigid with

tension. On his shoulder, his bird stalks back and forth shrieking unhappily as if she's trying to ward off attack.

I reach up and put a hand on his sleeve and when he meets my gaze, I say the only thing I can think of to keep him hopeful.

"We aren't without allies, Stekkan."

"Of course," he says but he doesn't sound like he believes me. "I suppose we have the spirits in our swords."

I force myself to lift my chin and feign confidence. "And we have my father. Admiral Redtide, the Hound of the Seas."

He looks at me and frowns. "What good is he so far away?"

"Ships sail," I say firmly. "And soon his will return. And when it does, we will have our ally."

I don't know if it helps, but I wait for him to leave before I let my shoulders slump and my forehead fall forward. What are we going to do? What could we possibly do?

This is where a real monster hunter would be helpful. But since there is only me, I need a plan. And it would be helpful if I could come up with it before my king returns with his anxious eyes and certainty that I can find the solutions to his problems. I need Vargaard.

CHAPTER TWO
NAKURAKI

The moment I'm drawn back into the Sea of Shadows, I sense a change within the raging tide of damned souls. There is a ... lessening. Any change in this grim place leaves me prickling with anxiety. This is not a place where change is ever good.

I climb atop the shoulders and heads of others, hardening my heart to their cries and fury, and once I am as high as I can manage atop a wobbling tower of bodies, I see far enough that the rift is visible, and the tide of the dead washes out over it. What heart I still have squeezes within me for this is worse than the worst that we feared. The longer this rift remains open, the longer the souls within can wash out into the world beyond.

Already, we are outnumbered and overwhelmed. Betrayed by our leaders. Those who are evil are willing to unleash violence and depravity on the innocent, and the innocent are intent on rescuing the weak and small and so unable to fight back blow for blow. How shall we stand against such bitter odds?

I am still swallowing down a rising tide of bleak despair when my name calls me out. Calls me back to her — she who is my heart. My home.

CHAPTER THREE

Vargaard appears again in my shadow and with me sitting on the ground, there is not much of one. He must tuck in tight beside me by force of his limitations.

"I can't leave you. Do not ask it of me".

His words are in my mind almost immediately, before I can even turn my face to look at him. They're tense and ground out like his mind is full of glass.

"I thought you were planning to leave me to go and hunt Nakuraki," I whisper. And I do everything I can to make sure my voice comes out neutrally, not plaintive or accusative. "Why this sudden shift of heart?"

He makes a chopping motion with his shadow hand, his brow furrowed and flickering in what looks like indecision.

"This is not what I mean. To cross over with the Fisher King is to leave this life forever. That's not an option."

I try to be gentle and I fight down a lump in my throat

as I also try to be unselfish. I'm not very good at unselfish-
ness, it would seem.

"You would cross to the lands beyond where you will
see your mother and sisters. You are meant for that,
Vargaard. You have proven yourself again and again. You
are the best of men and you deserve the best of futures."

His shadowed eyes trace my face and his hand comes
up to cup my cheek, unfelt but there. He meets my gaze
and his own almost feels violent, harsh, as if he is waging a
war against me.

"Would you be rid of me then, Vali?"

I shake my head violently enough that my tears flick
out like rain. I'm crying but I don't mean to be. It's hard to
keep emotions this powerful from creeping into everything. They exhaust me even when they come in tiny drops
and flickers.

"We must be practical, my shadow guardian. Look
around you. I am broken. I cannot even run to safety. I
certainly cannot fight any longer."

My words make his shadow flicker from Vargaard to
Vargaard, more quickly than ever, but I press on. I think I
have distressed him, but we must have this talk.

"My nation is conquered. There is no way to rouse a
proper defense now. Even the arrival of my father in his
ships cannot be enough, though I have offered it as hope to
our new king because I have nothing else to give him."

He's shaking his head and parting his lips to speak, but
I press on.

"Perhaps the King could tuck me back into his gem
and clutch his invisibility sword and walk us away from

here, but by three days' time from now — long enough to get to the borders by horse — every nation surrounding us will be infected by this plague. They will fall as we have. We cannot raise an army to fight. We cannot protect the living innocents who remain. Perhaps we could hide. Perhaps. But I was there with you in the Sea of Souls and I know what grim fate we would face remaining within it for months or years or decades."

"*What are you saying, Ilsaletta?*" he asks me tenderly. And in his baritone voice I hear the echoes of my wistful heart.

"I am telling you not to shackle yourself to me. Go back into the Sea of Souls and let the Fisher King bear you to the Beyond. There is no hope for us, here. No escape. Don't stay here with me as I fall and die before this horde."

He's shaking so hard that he keeps dissolving into shadow only to return again, bursting and coalescing only to burst again. His thoughts reach my mind in jagged shreds.

"*You* are *my life.*"

"But perhaps I should not be."

"*You hold my heart.*"

"You could take it back."

"*I will not go.*"

"What if you miss your chance?"

He bites his lip, wild-eyed. "*Speak plainly. Is this what you mean or do you disguise other feelings?*"

"What other feelings would there be?" I hiss. I think I hear rustling in the trees behind us, but I can barely shift my weight to ease discomfort and pain, never mind looking for possible enemies. I am vulnerable here.

"Do you despair of life and seek your own death?"

"No." My answer is small. I wish I could turn all this back and never have to live any of it after finding him.

"Do you wish you'd been wise enough to marry your duke and now you see this is still a possibility? The pair of you could reign and rule over two countries."

There's no bitterness in his voice, only grim practicality.

"I do not."

"Do you then find yourself smothered by my presence, appalled by my lack of courage when the tide washed over us, worried that if you take me in hand I will snap in your grip?"

"Of course not." Now, he is irritating me. I am not so inconstant. "But why should you suffer for nothing? Why should you die and gain nothing for your sacrifice? Go while you still can. Take the Fisher King's offer and *live.*"

He flings himself onto one knee before me.

"I meant the vows I said when first I gave myself to you. I did not think you would need reminding, but I remind you now." And suddenly he presses a fist to his heart, his eyes fiery and expression severe. *"In your shadow may I dwell that your shadow I may be. Your sorrows I will borrow. Your pain I will bear. The lifting of your head shall be my glory. The light of your eyes my delight. To the last drop of my blood I will defend you. Screaming defiance into the depths. And if I fail in my vow, may curses fall on my head and may my soul walk the howling roads beyond the veil."*

I think it already has.

"Then I know that of which I speak." His tone sounds final. Determined. Possibly a little furious. *"I will be your man beyond the bonds of the Nakuraki vow. I will be yours to the marrow until long past the days your frame has graced this earth. I am yours in every sense that word has ever held."*

"You've already given me all of that," I remind him gently. "I'm not asking for more. I'm giving you the chance to offer less."

"Take my soul, too." His eyes look desperate.

"I will not," I whisper as if it is my own vow. "I will not take from you what is most precious. I want the best for you, my Vargaard. I want you to find happiness and peace someday and I do not see how you could find them with me."

"I do not see how I could find them without *you,"* he snarls.

"Then we are at an impasse." I offer him a weak smile but I have not fought alongside him this long to just let him give up everything for me without even a fight. I steel my jaw, though I am trembling. I will fight for his future even if he will not. "Perhaps, for now, we should turn our great minds to the problem at hand. If I cannot win, then perhaps we can make them bleed as we die."

He looks away, still trembling with emotion, his shadow flickering so quickly that it makes me ill.

"I will win," he assures me. *"Perhaps you will not save everyone, but I can still save you."*

I bite my lip and look at him and for a moment I do

not feel the pain in my side and leg because the pain in my heart is too great.

To think of life without my shadow guardian is like looking on Swordheart as she fell. Bleak, agonizing, hopeless.

But to think of him losing his eternal future for me, damning himself to the mortal plane, or worse, to the Sea of the Souls — forever in the morass of cast-offs — this cuts me to the very soul. It's hard to breathe for a moment. Hard to think. I cannot force his hand on this, but I cannot delight in how he has cheated himself by choosing me.

"Let's read the book," I offer, "and as we read it, perhaps you can explain to me what you meant when you said you might have to leave me — before you chose to stay with me when you should have left with the Fisher King."

I open *The Grimoire of Souls and their Magic* and I try to ignore the faraway shouts in the distance, and instead, I balance the book on my knees and try to squint into the moonlight. I cannot see well enough to read. It's only when I give up that I realize he has not spoken.

I cock my head to the side and consider him and he knows I'm watching. He refuses to speak, simply flickers like a heartbeat.

"Where were you planning to go?" I ask him gently.

I can see his full body sigh before he finally collapses and admits, *You remember Stekkan's talk of a white lady? The one who gave him tranquility and explained things to him?*

"Yes."

"I have seen this lady in the Sea of Souls just as I have

seen all the others at one time or another — whether afar or right under my foot and fist. Some sleep, but others await within the chaos of the Sea. "

"And is it your idea to go in after them?

He looks nervous, but still, he answers. *"Yes. I see no choice. If you wish to gather the swords, then their masters are unlikely to free them and they'll be well guarded. I must find them on this other plane. "*

Behind his shadow, a crow flies up with a squawk. His last words are choked as he hovers over me, shadow sword in his hand, eyes flicking from bush to bush. I swallow down nervousness.

"You would go into the Sea of Souls on this mission alone?" I am careful in how I say it so that he will not shade his words to comfort me.

"I see no other way. If the enemy has the swords and the Nakuraki, then we cannot win. And if you are determined to see me go — then I should go in a way that helps you. "

I do not let him draw me into that. I do not like his plan — mostly because it involves him taking all the risks while we wait here for him.

"You're determined to take this path?" I press.

He nods and his shadow flickers quickly from Vargaard to Vargaard even as he spins in a slow circle.

"I'm surprised you don't have a story to tell me about how some past Vali allowed this and you won a great victory," I say wryly.

His half-smile matches mine. *"Alas, all my stories are fleeing me as the birds fly up from the fox. "* He pauses. *"Your king is quick. I see him riding this way. "*

I swallow and force myself to my wobbling feet. My leg is going to continue to be a problem. Perhaps Stekkan, too, would be better free of me.

"Please, won't you go back into the sea and give yourself to the Fisher King?" I beg one last time and he bursts apart twice before he can pull himself together enough to plead with me.

"Do not ask this of me, book girl. Ask me, instead, to help you save the world."

"I do not want to do that."

"Ask me to never leave you."

"I will not."

I will not love myself more than him. I look away, refusing to meet his eye.

I hear his choking gasp.

His words leave me hollow. *"You know I have no heart but if I did, it would beat for you."*

"You know I have no future, but if I did I would give it up if only you could have one, too," I choke out but I won't look at him. I can't.

"I will give you one", he says and it sounds like a curse and then he shatters into fluttering shadows and is gone.

The pounding hooves of the horses Stekkan is bringing set a quiet thrum in my heart. I cling to it because I hate myself right now for not clinging to Vargaard, even while I am proud that I was steady enough to insist that he go. Perhaps, when he is offered a place again in paradise, he will not turn it down for me. Perhaps I will look back on this firm disagreement and remember only that he loved me and that we were once friends.

"Where is your shadow?" Stekkan asks worriedly when he arrives.

"Never far off." I do not feel as confident as I sound.

Stekkan swallows and dismounts quickly, his lithe form edged in bright moonlight. If I were to choose a storybook king from a line of men I would choose Stekkan every time. He makes helping an injured girl into a palfrey look like a kingly task.

"The monks are still in their tower," he says as he helps me up. "I bid them bar the door, but they did not listen. I think you and I could spend the night there if we must."

We exchange an uneasy look and I know if there were more light we would both look green in the face. After our last few encounters, neither of us wants to be near members of a faith. The evil in their midst is horrifying.

"They have pigeon cotes," he says quietly. "And the monastery makes records of any messages going to or from their cotes. They may have clues for us."

"Clues of what?" I ask grimly but Stekkan only shrugs. "Of whatever there is to find. I'll still save Greghoiren if I can."

"Did all of Jendaya's allies come with her to Swordheart?" I ask him.

He nods.

"A fast horse takes three days to reach the closest borders from here. If we can stop them in three days ..."

I let the words hang in the air. We both know it's impossible but eventually Stekkan hisses it to himself. "Impossible."

He sounds like his heart has been broken all over again.

"Impossible," his spirit macaw repeats miserably.

"I've seen many impossible things these last few days," I say with a hope I do not feel. But it's enough for Stekkan. He nods grimly and begins to set the pace toward the monastery.

"I will consult the white lady tonight," he says over our horses' hoof beats after a pause. "Perhaps she will know of a way to help."

"To gather the Nakuraki and end the plague?" I ask.

He barks a nervous laugh, looking around him. "No. She's not a goddess. I was hoping she'd know a way to speed the healing in your leg. We have no time to spare in hobbling or limping."

I snort at that. But it is one thing I like about Stekkan. He tends to stick to solving the problem right in front of him before worrying about other goals, and as the person who mainly benefits from that, I won't complain.

"Then I hope her wisdom abounds."

We ride as grimly as messengers of death and we do not stop until we reach the monk's door. I am just beginning to think of actual sleep and possibly a warm drink when a monk slips out the door and vomits, falling to his knees and clutching his head.

"Impossible," the spirit bird whispers. And her words are still echoing in my head when the monk's face splits in two and from the center, peach-colored smoke unfurls in curls and whorls and I realize that I've called Vargaard's name without intending to, but my shadow guardian is not there.

CHAPTER FOUR

I do not hesitate. I plunge the Mercy Sword into the monk's back while he is still blooming.

My leg bucks under me, slipping as it cannot bear the weight I put on it, and forcing me to clamp my lips tightly around the scream that wants to slip out. My eyes stream with the effort and I have to take little huffing breaths to manage the lancing agony rushing through my foot.

By the time I can open my eyes and steady my breath, the monk is pinned firmly to the ground, my blade straight through his back and heart.

I am both relieved and strangely horrified. I can kill on my own now, if my victim is obliging enough to bend over on all fours and expose his back first. It makes my stomach churn. I am no longer the girl with the wind in her hair and books in her arms.

I am beginning to become a monster hunter in truth.

"Well, monster hunter," Stekkan hardly even looks shaken as he glances from the dead monk to me and back.

He's tying the horses to a post beside their watering trough. And removing their tack with fast, practiced hands. "I was wondering whether you could kill when he isn't here. If there was truly nothing of the warrior in you then we would both be dead. It seems my question has been answered."

The smile he offers me is somewhat manic, but the bird on his shoulder shakes her head sadly and flutters her spirit wings.

"*Impossible,*" she spits.

"This might answer another question for us," I say looking from the grim sight below and then up at the smooth tower. There has been no cry of outrage from within. There should be. The night is black and sharp, clear as a polished crystal. There is no reason that they should not have sounded an alarm. In the distance, a bird screams an alert, and a dog barks hollowly. I swallow. "Had they heard of events in Swordheart before you arrived to borrow horses?"

"Not firsthand," Stekkan says, his eyes meeting mine. There's a bitterness and sorrow in them. I know it well.

"What did they say?"

"They'd had pigeons but this is a long way out from Swordheart and it is night. It is their custom to shut their doors in mid-afternoon for prayers and keep them shut until down the next morning."

"And did they open them for you?"

He nods but he won't meet my eye.

"Then we know now. We can carry the plague even though we are unaffected by it."

"Are we?" His eyes are suddenly on mine, his words a rush of tangled emotions fighting to spill out. "Are we unaffected? I do not feel like the same Duke who met you in Saltfast."

"That is because you are King," I say gravely. I must remain firm. I must not crumble or we are all lost.

His shaken head and scowl show exactly what he thinks of this, but I hobble forward, ignoring his churning emotions. What can I do about them? I cannot even sort out my own feelings about this terrible epoch of time. Who expects to live through the downfall of all of civilization? Not me.

"Or," he says, glancing fondly at his spirit macaw and trying in vain to stroke her spirit head, "or, the pigeons brought it hours ago."

"In which case, we have no hope of saving anyone," I say grimly.

"*Impossible,*" Mercy agrees gravely, flexing a single wing.

We enter the tower through the door the monk opened and I look at Stekkan, considering, before I bolt it behind us. Who knows what horrors we will face within? But they may well be better than what is without.

"We don't need to go in here," Stekkan whispers.

I do not whisper. Whispers sometimes carry further than low-spoken words.

"What alternative is there? I cannot walk or ride far. You have walked all night and been up for two days and nights without rest. This place is defensible."

The bottom of the tower and the main room of the monastery are the same. It extends out from it in a narrow rectangle with long boards and benches on either side. The far end of the long room is wreathed in shadows and likely holds an altar. The only light here is the moonlight splashing through the narrow slit windows. There are two slumped heaps on the floor in the middle. I need no one to identify the dead for me anymore.

Carefully, we move up the spiral stairs to the next level where a long hall runs over the worship and dining room below. There are small doors along it in either direction and candles burn in their sconces. We look at each other and grimace, but the task must be done. As quietly as possible, we move from room to room until we have confirmed that all but four of the beds are full and all of the occupants dead.

When we're done, Stekkan holds up one finger and I nod. It does not take us long to find the last monk. He is dead on the stairs leading to the top of the tower. We climb with as much haste as I can muster on a broken ankle and find the top of the tower open at the sides but with a roof, the bell neatly placed in the center, dove cotes to either side, feed for birds and water, and a long table with pens and scraps of paper and log book wait for us.

I both love and hate this as a spot to spend the night. It is, indeed, defensible. You can see who might approach in every direction. These are good things. But you can also hear everything and in the air of the warm night, I can hear distant screams and shouts and even see the glow of far-off Swordheart.

"I'll gather supplies quickly," Stekkan says with a

shudder and I grimace. "At least there was only one monk who was evil."

"I almost prefer the evil ones," I admit.

His face tells me he fears for my sanity.

"Think about it," I say grimly. "It's the other ones who have let this take place. They're to blame for the fall of my nation, and likely yours, too."

"They're dead, Ilsaletta. They don't *let* anything happen," Stekkan says dryly.

"They did it by not being good," I say fiercely. "By not being the type of people capable of standing up to evil. They left the rest of us to do it and there are not enough of us."

"I won't argue with that." He's gone before I hear the resignation in his voice. Have I broken Stekkan? I hope not. His blind faith in Ghregoiren and that bird are better than my cynicism.

I make my way to the log book and light the candle on the little table. Whichever dead monk — likely the one on the stairs — was responsible for this did an excellent job.

The logs are clear. They have received the warning of a plague and passed it on — though, obviously, they were not worried enough to keep Stekkan out. Perhaps they did not think it would spread so far and so fast. A message was received also that declared Jendaya Queen of Cragspear, married now to Stekkan Duke of Catterail, now King of Cragspear — and the language here suggested that she might have a claim on Ghregoiren through him — and sent her regrets on the death of her father to the surrounding nations with requests that fast ships be sent to the colonies and those nations we trade with across the sea.

It's that which still has me breathless when Stekkan emerges with a stack of folded blankets, a bottle of wine, and food.

"If we're going to die, let's eat first."

He makes a nest of blankets as I flip through the other messages.

"Jendaya has requested that fast ships be sent to all our allies to announce her ascension to the throne." My voice sounds as grey and dull as I feel.

"Grand. I'll just open this wine, shall I?"

"She also announces that she has wed a prince of Ghregoiren."

"Well, that's just lying now," he says and he smirks as he arranges the food he's brought for us. "I'm not sure that there's enough wine here and I brought four bottles. Here, you can have one and I'll see if the other three are enough to drown my princely sorrows."

My hand stills over the page. This message is from ... yesterday, maybe? Two days ago? I have to look at the jotted dates. My own mind has lost a lot of time. Oh, the third day of the Month of the Moth. And today ... no yesterday ... is noted as the seventh day of the Month of the Moth. This is four days ago.

"What has your attention seized by the throat?" My new-declared king is looking at me with wary eyes as he uncorks a bottle of wine.

"It is a message from the coast. Ships spotted, sporting the crest of my father's fleet."

He pauses, lowering the bottle in his hands. "How long ago?"

My mouth is dry as I meet his glittering brown eyes. "Four days."

His heart must be racing, too, because his breath is ragged now. "And how long after spotting them would they have made port?"

"It depends on where he chose to put in," I say in a strangled voice. "He might have gone home. And if he did it would have taken at least an extra day from when he was spotted — perhaps two."

"And if he made for Seamark, which is more likely with a full fleet?" Stekkan's hand tenses on his sword hilt. I do not know why. There's a strange glitter in his eye. By now you'd think I'd know him so well that nothing would surprise me, but this is Stekkan and he is by turns loyal and flagrant, optimistic and miserable. I can't read this look in his eye at all.

"He could have made port the same day he was spotted, or the next day. He could be three or four days in the country."

"Would he have gone to Saltfast to look for you when he saw that Seamark was devastated?" Oh. The glitter is hope. It is so unexpected that it steals my breath for a moment. I see it swelling up in his eyes even as I see him swallow, trying to force the emotion away.

"I think so," I whisper.

"So, a day spent journeying there, perhaps a day going back when he realizes you are not where he left you. Three days from Seamark to Swordheart by horse."

"He would not take a horse, I think," I say, twisting my fingers together. "He would take a river boat so he could bring as many of his men as he could."

Stekkan's eyes meet mine and our expressions both shift to misery at once. "And two in ten may still be alive of those he brings, and of those two, one will be bent on killing the other."

I swallow. I cannot find my voice.

"I will do you the honor of suggesting your father will live," he says and his voice comes out like a squeak. "I will even go so far as to assume he will not turn."

"Thank you," I say gravely.

But my mind is full of my father. His laugh. His kindnesses. Tiny treats slipped to me. Books read at bedtime. Maps poured over together. Trinkets brought from foreign places. Pipe tobacco, and mint, and spices from far away. His lined face weathered and smiling, always smiling when he looks at me. He'd have to be one of the few good men, would he not? Even Stekkan here — foppish and flighty as can be — he is good. Would my father not have to be good?

I sink deeper into his coat which is wrapped around me and my stomach twists so hard it's half in my throat. I'm bowled over with the desperate longing of homesickness but at the same time, I'm shredded with anxiety.

Because I don't know.

I've seen too much now to make assumptions about anyone. Anyone at all. I do not dare believe in the certainty that my father is a good man.

"How long is the journey by riverboat?" Stekkan asks, calmly.

I struggle to keep my inner turmoil out of my voice. "It's upstream and the river is fractious. It's no quicker than by horse."

He nods. "Then he is a day or two away at most. If he lives. If he came this way."

Our eyes meet and I know we are both balanced precariously together on the edge of hope and panic. And we don't dare panic. I muster the last of my strength and force a smile.

"What wonderful news. How is the wine, my liege?"

He manages a weak smile for that. "Not my preferred vintage, but even kings can't be too choosy."

I hobble over to the blanket to eat and drink my share in silence.

When I'm finished, Stekkan is still drinking, staring dolefully toward the distant screams. He says, "And now we need to talk about the White Lady."

CHAPTER FIVE

Stekkan draws his sword so suddenly that I flinch backward and he shakes his head. I see his hands are wrapped with a cloth like he's afraid to hold the hilt with the blade naked unless it is wrapped.

"I'm not talking to her myself just yet," he says, looking nervous. "But listen. I bolted the trap door to the levels below. We've eaten. We both need sleep."

In the distance, there is a sound that makes the floor rumble. I don't like it.

"We cannot stop whatever is out there," he continues and I think he's saying this for his own benefit because he isn't looking at me. "And we cannot flee it tonight. I can barely keep my eyes open. I have been awake for two days and nights straight, and have fought battles I never wanted to fight, and seen horrors that would shake a man made of sterner stuff than me. If I do not rest, I will melt like snow in springtime. And I'll probably have to drink a great deal of this wine to keep me from reliving the horrors I've seen as I sleep."

I nod my agreement, but I need sleep as well. He must see my thoughts in my eyes, for he clenches his jaw before he says, "Even though you also need rest, you need to be healed even more. I'll set your leg for you before I seek the blankets, but I think you should take the Tranquility Sword and consult with the lady. If she could tell me to put you in a gem, perhaps she knows how to ease your pain. She has knowledge beyond mortal reckoning."

"Oh, she'll ease it," I say with lips curling with disdain. "She'll make me tranquil and calm until I feel nothing, but I'll walk on a broken foot."

His lips form a firm line and I realize he's struggling to speak but when the words come to his lips I can see why this was hard for him. The fierce firmness of his words startles me.

"If she grants you the knowledge to heal a broken bone, then we are saved, for you will be able to travel and fight. But if she does not, then tomorrow you must ride with both swords in your grip and you must walk on your broken foot, and hope her tranquility keeps you from screaming, for we do not have any other choice."

I nod, quick and determined. This new Stekkan scares me. But he is not wrong. He sets his jaw and I see that it's taking all his mental strength to be firm with me. Stekkan is not naturally a taskmaster. He is no Vargaard to push me beyond my current strengths.

He works with the supplies he brought from below to set my ankle for me and then he drinks a long draught of the wine, takes a blanket, rolls himself in a ball like a beetle, and is asleep while I'm still getting comfortable enough to grab the sword and risk my fate with the lady.

She comes to me immediately while Stekkan snores, her white hands smoothing my hair and face, and though I know she is but a dream, and she cannot touch me at all, I still feel my heart fluttering in my chest as she calms my breathing and stills my juddering thoughts.

"Please," I say when I can finally find words. "Can you help me heal my bones?"

Her words take a long time coming, cloaked in white mist and cloudy thoughts, and I have the worst feeling that too much time is passing in the real world and that I am missing it here, but I cannot seem to make myself care enough to do anything about it. Tranquility has overtaken me as an enemy overtakes you in the night. It forces my gasping breath to slow, forces my racing pulse to calm.

"*Resonance,*" she breathes to me eventually. "*For each sword you acquire, there is resonance. They strengthen one another.*" She sighs happily. "*I feel the warm rush of peace.*"

The tranquility is so heavy that I can barely find a word to speak. But my slow thoughts are telling me she is correct. That this tranquility is heavier, thicker, than what I felt before when I drifted away with her.

"Then it will aid the Mercy Sword?" I eventually ask.

And it feels like a year before I hear her "*Yes.*"

And her thick tranquility has wrapped me up so I cannot hear or see. My mind is lost even to myself.

A rough hand shakes me and then the sword is dragged from my heavy grasp and I gasp in a sharp breath.

It's dawn.

Already.

I see the bright rays ripping through the sky and hear the birds singing their greeting. My heart jumps, suddenly bouncing from rib to rib in its shock. It's free of the grasp of Tranquility with a suddenness that makes it feel as though it might burst.

"It's morning," I hear myself say stupidly.

"Mercy," the spirit macaw agrees sadly.

My eyes focus and land on Stekkan's concerned face.

"Did you sleep at all?" he asks, sounding upset.

"Did you?" I ask in reply and my voice sounds rough and unused.

He opens his mouth to answer but then he shakes himself instead as if reminded that he was here for something else. "Healed or not, we must flee now. I hear the sounds of marching feet."

And he's right. Under the birdsong is the low thrum of thousands of feet hitting the earth. My spine shivers at the feeling of it and I pull myself to my feet. My ankle is tender but it takes the weight. I pull back the shoulder of my coat and see that my arm is completely healed.

Resonance. Her blade, working together with mine, has made me heal at an alarmingly quick rate.

"Yes," I say, and I call in my mind, *Vargaard?* and feel like sobbing when he does not come to me.

No, Ilsaletta. You wanted that for him. You wanted him to be free. Do not regret it now.

"Is it to be Ghregoiren or the river?" Stekkan asks me,

eyes intent. If he feels ill effects from his drinking last night they do not show.

I shake my head.

"You tell me, King of Cragspear," I say dryly.

"This is not for me to decide," he says, looking out from the tower bitterly. His face hardens at what he sees and I make my way carefully to where he stands, my grip tight on the Mercy Sword.

Something dark floods across the ground from the direction of Swordheart. On the road, it is most likely the army. It is their feet we hear marching, and this can only be Jendaya's pre-infected army — those already sifted by the plague of the green gem.

But it is the figures that rush over the hills and grass away from the roads that worry me. I fumble in the monks' things to find what I suspected must be there. A small looking glass. Held with care, it reveals my worse fears. Like bad food brought up in a flood, the land is awash with the tumult of the strange spirit creatures that poured from the gash Jendaya carved in the air.

If my heart was not sick within me before, it is quaking now.

"My land is lost," I say, the words fluttering from me like a broken flag. "My people have no chance of surviving this." I turn my eyes to his set features. "But Ghregoiren remains. And you have been elevated to king of Cragspear. So yes, actually, this is for you to decide. What shall we do next, Stekkan the Grim, King of Cragspear? Shall we run those two palfreys to death all the way to Ghregoiren and beg them seal their gates, and man their towers, and shall we name those who have betrayed them to their enemies, or shall we ride for the river, and follow her course in search of our last possible ally in this land — Admiral Redtide?"

He swallows visibly and I am struck again by what a contrast he is — fearful and yet driven to save his people. Helpless in the face of trouble, and yet he faced his every fear to bring back the spirit macaw who sits on his shoulder. And even now, rumpled, torn, bloodstained, and dirty, his beauty shines like the sun. He looks every inch the king. But over those hills, marching to tear us to pieces, is his queen. And she will show no mercy.

"You could read the book," he says grimly. "You *should* read the book."

"The army will be here within hours," I say, studying them again through the glass. "Even if we ride now, we will hardly have time to warn anyone."

"I chose the road to Ghregoiren to flee down," he says with a rough laugh. "What a fool I am. Of course they march this way."

"Jendaya has likely sent armies and representatives in every direction," I say calmly.

"Every direction except south. What need has she to reconquer what has already been taken? Had I chosen south over east, we could be well on our way toward your father."

"With no knowledge that he is even here."

He nods at my assessment, accepting it. He needs to make this choice. I don't know why I know it, but I do.

To my surprise, he turns to me and his brow furrows. "Where did your spirit guardian go?"

"I do not know," I say, feeling worry lace through me. "But I know he had plans to ... to try to hunt down the others trapped in their swords."

He swallows, nodding his head. "Has he ever been gone this long?"

"Yes. When he was mortally wounded."

His grimace tells me he understands our exact situation. "Neither you nor I are warriors on our own. And we have already seen what happens when we try to outrun this plague. We will not try to out-race them to Ghregoiren. We will search instead for your father. Any ally right now is more than we two have between us."

I look away because it is now my turn to face grim facts. "And if he has turned? Or is dead?"

Stekkan shrugs. "Then Divine Sovereign have mercy on us."

"*Mercy,*" echoes the macaw. She stoops down and tries to take a bite of his hair, screeching angrily when she cannot grasp it.

"We'll ride double," Stekkan decides. "I will watch for trouble and you will study that book. If there is salvation for any of us, it's not in flight or warnings. We've learned that much. But perhaps there is another way."

CHAPTER SIX
NAKURAKI

I cannot lift myself from the depths. Feet press onto every part of me, every limb, every inch of my body, and head. My face is trodden upon again and again. The Sea of Souls surges and I am rolled under her tide. I found them here — clustered together, standing in a ring back to back. They are unworried by the changes in the sea. Certainly unconcerned by me.

They laughed and taunted when they caught sight of me and then two of them broke from the cluster and we danced the grim dance of death and pain.

Haszinth, sixth of his name, rides upon a farrakki, a strange creature made of shuffling, shifting bones, never quite one thing or another. Beside him, a second Nakuraki charges at me, a man made of woven whips, his hair braided into seven whip-like braids. The Akul Khanani who I glimpsed before.

I do not think we will persuade these Nakuraki to help us defeat the Scourge. I do not think they can be reached at all. They want only destruction, revenge, and escape. And would I be one of them had I not woken to my Ilsaletta's need? Would I seek any escape I could find even if it meant dancing in the ashes of the world?

I fought well. I fought hard, but in the end, I was bested and broken, left with pieces carved away, crippled by agony, abandoned to be trampled beneath the sea. I have seen souls in this state. I have seen as the years melt one to another and still, they do not pull themselves up, as I cannot pull myself up now.

I hear her call to me, my sun, my stars, but I cannot go to her. I cannot so much as flicker. I wish for eyes that I may cry for her. I wish for a voice that I might bid her flee. I am a drowned soul, churned under, washed away.

CHAPTER SEVEN

Stekkan is an able horseman. I've noted it before but it bears mentioning again as he leads us through the little low points between the hills and off the roads and trails men would use. We are riding double on one horse as he leads the other so that we might switch horses when the first is tired. We have brought little with us from the monastery. If we live long enough to eat the bread, we will have done very well.

I ride before him so that I can spread the book out over the horse's neck. He has stolen the exact one that we need, it would seem. Even in pain from my ankle, with the sounds of pursuit behind us, and operating on very little sleep, I am riveted to the pages.

The Grimoire of Souls and their Magic is full of careful ink drawings of its contents, which makes it both horrifying and fascinating in equal measure.

I am desperate to find answers within. So desperate that my hands tremble as they stroke the ragged edges of the vellum pages. Will I find a way to destroy my enemies? Can I possibly turn back this flood of the dead sweeping over my land?

I am anxious to the point that my own thoughts are laced with acid. I have never gone so long without Vargaard unless he was injured. Surely some harm has befallen him, but where he has gone, I cannot follow, and I fear that he is alone and can only save himself. The thought of it makes my entire body twist and ache.

"How much of this did you read?" I whisper to Stekkan as we ride.

"Enough," he says directly into my ear and I nearly jump.

The beginning is well enough. The author natters on about the theory of soul and body and how they are interwoven. In his mind, we are all connected to a great group of souls on another plane. Well and good. We are, after all, able to enter the Sea of Souls when we have died or when some nefarious person banishes us there. I found it myself when I was tucked away into the amulet.

I skim a little, not worried about how he reached these conclusions. It's more the results I'm after. I have a shadow guardian to find and draw back, swords to gather, and a host of enemies to defeat.

He moves from there to a consideration of the ethics of tampering with souls and with tapping them, twisting them, changing them to produce the power of magic. For someone who has brought to our attention that there might be an ethical problem here, he seems very at peace with potential consequences. He seems, one might argue, eager to try his hand at it and is merely excusing himself and his ambitions in these pages.

I flip through them but I stop when we reach his account of his first trials. They are grisly indeed.

I flip further. And here is where I find he has succeeded in his attempt to trap a soul — aided, it would seem by an ancient artifact he has found — a green gem. This must be the Scourge of Stolen Heights. Our author notes how he has brought together seven swords of varying origins. How old is this book?

He has determined it is to these swords he shall affix spirits and he shall somehow imbue them with magic stolen from the artifact — or perhaps the trapped soul? He rambles here as if uncertain about how exactly to achieve his goal.

My hands are shaking as I read. This book is about the origins of the Nakuraki and if I need all seven to defeat Jendaya and her Scourge, then isn't this the exact information that I need?

But this book can't be old enough to have been written before the Nakuraki were created. I flip back to the beginning and I find what I'm looking for. A record that shows the book translated and translated again, scribed and transcribed through the ages, until a monk in my grandfather's time adapted the language for ease of reading. Beside his name and notes, is a different hand that records the date of his death and is initialed. My heart freezes within me for I am no fool. I can see what happened here.

"I think it was seeing how they were killing the scribes that first caught my attention, too," Stekkan says from over my shoulder. "What is so sensitive that it requires the deaths of any who ever saw it?"

"Something kept in a vault by the kings of Cragspear and foolishly left where your wife could find it and turn it to her will," I say tightly.

"The same could be said about me, except for the vault part," Stekkan mutters, but I have already turned back to my search.

I can hardly bear to read these horrific accounts. This man may style himself as a philosopher but his accounts of what he has done — how he has tapped into human bodies and against their will extracted their souls and placed them within these swords — makes him more of a demon in my mind.

He is vague about the details, as if to protect his new craft from replication.

That he has killed living people and destroyed their futures is not of consequence to him. And no one holds him to account, though he does not explain why. Perhaps he ruled a land or was so powerful that none dared judge him.

He does, however, explain that he took the souls out of his victims.

"Each one winnowed down to a single trait and that trait magnified and refracted when placed within the blade. Take for instance the Tenacity Sword. The Ghuhul" I think that means spirit, or ghost, "made Nakuraki for this blade was an unstoppable force, unwilling to so much as bend even as we stripped her of all humanity. That tenacity was boiled down, solidified, and imbued upon the blade so that now any who holds it, holds within himself a mighty perseverance and takes from his enemy all will to carry on."

I grimace. Hopefully, we would not be on the bad end of that sword. To lose the will to go on? That would be worse than any wound that could be inflicted.

What did it say about Vargaard that he was attached to the Mercy Sword. Had he been distilled until there was just one trait left in him, and it was compassion for others? I swallow hard at this thought, for I can tell just by its flavor that it is truth. Was he not there for me in my weakest moment?

"I removed each soul by use of the artifact," our horrific author writes.

The artifact. The green gem, if the sketches are to be believed, is the source of our plague.

And it does remove souls, doesn't it? But only from the truly evil. It splits open their faces and their souls puff up into smoke. Or, it leaps from chest and fingers in the form of fantastical glowing creatures. That can only be their souls twisted by magic, right? Perhaps, it is still operating as it did when it made the Nakuraki, only in an altered manner.

Does that make all of them Nakuraki of a sort? Boiled and distilled but not quite so thoroughly? Perhaps it is the similarity of a bowl of grapes left out until they rot compared to a fine wine carefully fermented.

"The swords form a sort of a trap," he writes. "Carved from the bones of a plane beyond, where the spirit takes flight after this life, they are one with that beyond world and so when the soul escapes the body, it is possible to divert it to the sword instead of to that great sea, and to lock it within by use of binding vows. These vows could perhaps be replaced if the soul were to give that same vow to another person or object and mean it with their whole self, consequences notwithstanding. But what fool would do such a thing? Damn himself to a breakable urn or to a mortal who will take ill and die? My Nakuraki are not so foolish. And — beyond that — ignorance is a gift. They do not know there is a means of escape."

Vargaard knew somehow. Or suspected. Or simply acted on impulse and lucked out.

"It takes two or three days for the soul to stick. It is true that some of the Nakuraki witnessed this with the others. But it would take a great mind to parse this, to work it backward, and see the door to escape."

I am forced to pause at this and I do not realize that Stekkan has paused with me, drawing our palfrey under a tree to hide from sight until he whispers in my ear.

"Did he give such vows to you, Ilsaletta?"

"He did," I say and I can hardly believe it. I knew he had abandoned the sword and entered my shadow instead. I knew he had changed the course of his future to mine. That he was no longer immortal as a result, but seeing it laid out so clearly is a shock. When he says he is mine, he means it utterly. While the other Nakuraki are reborn again and again, his star is ever fixed on me.

I must find him. I must draw him back to me.

"You're trying to collect all seven of these swords," Stekkan whispers in my ear. "And you're doing it because my queen told you that they could together bring about her downfall. But what if she was lying even then? What if she is merely trying to collect them for herself to increase her power."

That did sound very like Jendaya.

"What if what you actually need to do is destroy them? Have you noticed her power seems to increase with the more of them that she finds? And she certainly is intent on finding them."

He is making a lot of sense.

I swallow and read on, but Stekkan's hand is placed over mine when I move to turn a page and his finger finds my lips to silence me. The sound of other horses is clear. Stekkan has hidden us in bushes beside a babbling stream. It hides us well, but not well enough. I hear a snort as a horse draws near and a faint whicker.

I find my eyes wandering back to the words I just read.

"We chose the best of those we could find — warriors who fought to the last defending their people, mothers who offered themselves in place of their children, kings and queens of nations taken by the sword. We opened them up like the pages of the book and spliced them. With each one we forged, it only strengthened the power of the artifact ... or so we thought.

"In the end, we filled all seven swords. It was an arduous process, leaving more than a thousand corpses and weary scholars in our wake. They called my home the Altar of Agony after that. But I finally had all seven. And somehow, together, they were stronger than they could be apart. I had a harness crafted to hold them all across my back. But even that was not enough to sate my lust for them. I made them ring me like dogs, to leap and roll at my command."

I shiver at the words, even though they are thousands of years old and translated ten times.

"With their power, we created the Farrakki and scourged our enemies and when my Nakuraki died, they were reborn again and again within their swords. A guard may give his life for you once and be grateful. A Nakuraki may give it a thousand times and thank you for it.

"But we did not account for the artifact. We did not yet see the flaw in what we had wrought."

The hooves creep closer, tack jingling. I shift my hands from the book, to the hilt of the Mercy Sword and draw it as quietly as I can. Stekkan's free hand grips my hip in fear.

I close the book with great care but I might be too late.

In the leaves ahead of us, five horses step out.

CHAPTER EIGHT

A man in a stained cloak too ornate to be anything other than the trappings of the powerful rides to the stream where he allows his horse to drink. The horse is dappled in sunlight and shadow and the combination makes my mind race with half-formed thoughts. I bite my lip nervously. Beside the first rider, his noble companions to either side water their mounts, too. The others with him must be guards. They watch the trees, eyes flicking from shadow to shadow, horses jumpy, too. One of them is drumming his fingers on his sword hilt, but for some reason, they have not yet seen us.

I shift in the saddle. Five. If Vargaard were here, he could easily defeat all five, I think. With only the two of us, we are no match for this party.

"I don't think we'll find them to the south," one of the companions says cautiously. He flicks his hand out shivering and grimacing as if he just had a bucket of ice water dumped into one ear, and a bright blue cloud of smoke bursts from his wrist, forms a stallion, and rears in the air. He keeps it close, hunched over himself. He's more nervous than his words betray.

The powerful man seems to shrug, though it's hard to tell from where we are hiding. Even harder when he waves his hand idly and a yellow smoke tiger paws the air and dances around the horse. He watches it uneasily, clutching his lower belly as if letting out this smoke beast makes him ill — or gives him pain?

"It's what the queen has requested and we will do our job thoroughly," he says, swallowing visibly. He really is ill. "Search every building right down to the outhouses. Set men to check haystacks and lofts."

"Ilsaletta," Stekkan breathes into my ear. "Take my sword."

He reaches around me and with the most aching slowness, he draws the book from my lap and into his free arm. I have grown used to Stekkan and he seems to regard me as slightly less important than his dead bird. Even so, the brush of his hands on my thighs makes me feel too warm. I worry about what Vargaard will think when he returns. He already scorns the Duke ... King. Will he feel betrayed that we two have guarded each other's backs?

"We've been doing all that and more," the female companion says from by the river. If she has a smoke spirit to fight for her, then she isn't playing with it like the men are. That's likely wise if it hurts as much as it looks.

The whole group is young. Hardly older than I am. Their leader has the soft look of one who has only just learned to shave his whiskers.

The woman keeps speaking, as Stekkan and I make our awkward swap. "All we've found is bodies or peasants huddling in little knots. I don't like killing peasants. Where do you think our food comes from? You won't find me pushing a plow next spring."

I slide the Mercy Sword slowly from my scabbard, very careful not to make a sound.

"It's Cragspear's Queen's orders," the first man says. "Not for you to question."

Stekkan takes my other hand and places it on his sword hilt, urging me with a very intense look and a head nod to take it, too. I do not want to release his white lady before I must.

"But you already have a sword of your own, Count, not like that fool General Suavenfoil," the lady companion is saying in the clearing. The yellow tiger stalks toward her and she freezes, head held high, but face pale.

"Maybe I want two," the count says holding his pale chin high. The shadows under his eyes are growing darker by the moment. "Maybe I know things I can *do* with two."

"Maybe *you* can do things with them," Stekkan whispers in my ear. "Like hunting those monsters for us both. With the Tranquility Sword, you could be invisible."

He's not wrong, but I still swallow down uncertainty. I have not trained with Vargaard for very long. Invisibility may not be enough to save me if I try to fight anyone who knows what they're doing and those guards certainly look able.

"Won't you have to give it to the Queen?" The girl

makes her voice sound flippant, but even from here, I can tell she's scared.

"Yes, he certainly would," a voice tinkles as three more horses break through the trees. Two of the horses are carrying more guards. These ones are dressed in Cragspear royal livery. Very few of the guard survived Jendaya's overthrow of the throne. A fact I still find telling.

The last rider is Stekkan's wife.

Jendaya, Queen of Cragspear.

On her back is a scabbard and her sword handle juts up from it. Her marvelous golden curls are woven into a crown on her head and a real crown with three spikes in the front sits in place on top of the braids. She is every inch the queen, as she always has been, the only thing that would make you doubt it is the turquoise unicorn that paces around and around her as her smile goes colder and colder.

"Perhaps," the count says, turning his horse so he can face the queen, head held high. "Or perhaps when I deliver her runaway husband, she'll offer the sword as a reward?"

Jendaya laughs and her laugh is the only ugly thing about her. It rips harshly through the count's attempted titter. "If you think my husband is worth even half what one of those swords is, then you fool only yourself, Count Landsdown and you might as well return to Triverge and leave one of your companions in your stead. No? Then enough foolish talk. You'll bring me both sword and king and you'll do it before we find Admiral Redtide ... or we will revisit the idea of your replacement."

Stekkan's hand grips me so tightly now that discomfort has turned to pain, but I do not stop him.

"Please," he begs me, his whisper so faint I barely hear him. "Please Ilsaletta. You know I need her dead."

I need her dead, too. We all do. But Vargaard would tell me not to go rushing into danger with no plan. And my own heart might remind me that murder under any name is not for those who consider themselves good — not even if it is the most expedient option. But Vargaard is not here and Stekkan is convincing.

The spirit bird stares at me as if she can dive into my head and take over my reluctant body. Fortunately for us both, she says nothing, merely spitting at me with her spirit beak.

Stekkan grips my hand on the hilt of the sword. The moment seems to last forever. His inhale is long as it draws into his lungs, pupils dilated in eyes laced with black lashes. His full lips tremble. The vulnerability in his face is a shocking contrast to the scrape down one cheek that is healing in a rough, disregarded way.

He leans in so close that if we were lovers he might kiss me. He smells of horse and fear and very faintly of pears — which is very Stekkan — and he softens his whisper to something I think sounds more akin to the sounds of a bedroom than a forest mere paces from the enemy and his begging is so artful that even with all my defenses up, it twists at something low in my belly.

"Do this for me, Ilsaletta, and I will give myself to you utterly."

I swallow hard. I don't answer him. Not because I plan to take him up on that offer, but because I do not. It is bad enough that he has vowed to stay with me always. I will never ask him to lower himself in this way, too.

I break the tether our eyes have created between them and slide his blade from the sheath and the way his eyelashes flutter when I do it is nearly indecent. He wants revenge as some men want women. Or perhaps not revenge. With him and Jendaya, it's less than that and more than that, all tangled up in twisted love-hate misery. He's her victim and betrayer, lover and captive all in one and I don't really know if he's ever sure which he is in which moment.

The moment the blade is free I'm gripped by the White Lady, but this time I come with purpose and I force my legs to drop me to the ground, slow and careful. I do not feel the pain in my ankle with a sword in either hand, but I do call to my Nakuraki. Perhaps he can still hear me somehow, even if I cannot hear him.

What I am about to do, I do unselfishly, I tell him in my mind. *And I hope that you can forgive me.*

My heart is in my throat as I edge through the bushes — slowly, carefully.

Make me invisible, I plead with the white lady.

I do not know if she complies, but no one has raised an alarm or asked me to declare myself and I am nearly out from under the tree. I feel ... terribly calm ... as I grip the Tranquility Sword in my left hand. It is as if all of this is happening to someone else and not to me at all.

I draw in a long cleansing breath. I am the feather. I drift on the wind.

"Yes, you do," the White Lady tells me.

I let out a long slow breath and step out from beneath cover, placing my feet with great care so as not to rustle a leaf or crunch a branch.

Those before me continue their prattle. I do not hear their words. I am a feather.

No, the lady tells me. *You are a cloud. They cannot even touch a cloud. You float on tranquility.*

I float on tranquility.

I feel as though I am feverish. I see my enemies there — eight bodies. Eight souls. Eight horses. Those poor creatures. But their words come from far away.

"When you find my husband," Jendaya is saying and her words are slow and elongated as if she is speaking from underwater. The whole world is white, white, white as if I drift through mist. "Do not hurt him. But if anyone is with him, kill them."

It won't matter. They will not find Stekkan. They will not find me.

I am the cloud.

I step softly to the very center of the circle they have formed with their horses.

In my right hand, the Mercy Sword is ready to fight.

I inhale a long breath and find my balance, my center. The breeze ripples my hair. I am one with it, too. I open my eyes as wide as they will go, smile angelically, and step towards Jendaya, sword already in motion at the same moment that her hand brushes her sword hilt — by accident, I think — and her Nakuraki, Haszinth, sixth of his name, pours out, screaming like the bell on the top of a tower and as if a spell has been broken, they both inhale as one.

I know at once that they have seen me.

Jendaya twists and my blow comes down on the neck of her horse instead of on her. The blade sticks. I fight it even as the screaming horse falls to his knees and the Queen's unicorn shoots toward me. I must abandon the Mercy Sword to raise the Tranquility Sword in time to turn the creature's attack. It rears, its cries ripping through the air like a chorus of souls screaming in the Sea of Souls itself.

Jendaya has scrambled somewhere out of sight. Her companions freeze, gaping at her with open mouths, their horses dancing and shaking their heads with nervousness, as if the animals can see what is happening here even though the humans cannot.

I spin, looking for Jendaya, and barely get my blade up in time to turn a blow meant for me from her Nakuraki. His shadow blade crashes onto the Tranquility Sword so hard that it pushes it backward to bite into my own shoulder.

Not again.

My breath saws in my lungs. I am burning pain and flashes of wild visions. I swing out wildly, the laughter of the Nakuraki ringing in my ears as I miss. I reach down and rip my Mercy Sword free, but now a second Nakuraki sweeps forward and this one holds her head up high and extends a hand toward me.

And extends it...

And extends it past the point a human hand would

end, as it elongates like pulled cheese stretching, and shoots toward me.

I open my mouth to scream and then a shadow is there, slashing the hand from the shadow arm and spinning to grab Haszinth by his neck, wringing it as a farmwife wrings the necks of fowl.

My Vargaard has come.

CHAPTER NINE

Vargaard twists around me, his blows quick and precise. He is flowing shadow and darting blade. He turns Haszinth's blows one after another, in a rolling manner that feels like a baker twisting braided bread. He's lightning fast, his shadow-hair wild and flickering garments tattered. There is something untamed about his eyes as he moves, as if he floats on the very edge of sanity. I follow in his wake, clinging to the Tranquility and Mercy Swords.

He's back! He's here! Just the thought of it makes my heart leap.

What madness have you brought us into, book girl? He shoots a wild-eyed look at me but I'm too desperately happy to have him back to even answer.

How do I keep him with me?

I do not know.

How did I call him back?

I do not know that, either. I know only that anytime I hear your call I will move the Sea of Shadows itself to come to you. Your call can no more be denied than the calls of my own spirit.

The fancy fellow who first came down to the water holds a blade with a double cross-guard and it is this blade from which the female-looking spirit dances. Her eyes are wide, arms reaching out as if she will embrace the whole world. I can tell at once that he can see me, just as Jendaya can. Perhaps possessing a sword with a Nakuraki gives you eyes to see them. I can find no other way to account for how only those two can see what is happening.

I tried to hunt them in the Sea of Shadows, Vargaard tells me as he spins a cloverleaf pattern around me, disarming two enemies and then leaping back into his fight with Haszinth.

"Of course you failed to kill us within the Sea," Haszinth says and I gasp. He can hear us speak together?

Vargaard growls, "*I was not trying to kill them.*"

But Haszinth has more to say, "We are of one accord there, Nakuraki. That you are not, is a terrible aberration. But not for long. Our mistress will take your sword and join you to the rest of us."

At least they do not know all our tricks.

Hold fast, book girl.

I want more answers, but I do not want him to give them to me before our enemies' ears. I grip my sword handles tight and focus on staying at the ready, my attention on the whole scene around us while it is also narrowed down to any potential threats.

The other retainers and guards are in a panic, dancing back from blows they cannot see, but which still leave slashes if they get too close to Vargaard and Haszinth or even me. I swing at the second Nakuraki with the Tranquility Sword, blocking a furtive blow she sends out as if testing me. My block misses her, but bites into one of the guards and I see firsthand how the Tranquility Sword operates as it steals all calm from him, sending him immediately into panicked flight. His horse rears, catching fear from him, and then stomps forward, the edges of both forehooves catching another horse and rider, spreading the panic further.

"This is the problem we face," Vargaard says and frustration laces his tome. *"Together they are stronger than alone. Too strong."*

But so are we.

Haszinth's laughter echoes at that.

Half of those present are panicked or stampeding now, and still, I have not landed a proper blow.

Jendaya lets her unicorn loose and it leaps from her hand toward Vargaard. He turns the charge but has to respond with inhuman speed. The unicorn is quick and powerful.

The chaos is the only thing keeping me free of the third Nakuraki. She circles us with bright eyes, but fortunately, both times she has moved to leap toward me, a guard or retainer who is blind to her steps between us or knocks into her wielder, sending his sword's shadow wide of the mark. I keep the tips of my swords up, waiting, and I keep moving. The swords are clearly feeding from each other, even with only four of them present. I can see how this new sword fuels the strength of the Tranquility Sword, sending horses and riders into unimaginable panic with the barest touch.

Someone sounds a horn and a roar fills my ears. My own pulse deafens me as fear floods through my veins.

We are not making progress. Haszinth is too fast for Vargaard to pin in place.

My Nakuraki weaves and spins, twisting to lay his blade between me and danger again and again. I turn the blows of the third Nakuraki, but I do not have enough skill to strike back. She laughs a little hysterically as if she is barely holding on to sanity.

I can feel the question Vargaard asked burning a hole into my chest. Why had I agreed to try this? Could I not see it was folly?

The third Nakuraki leaps forward suddenly and I am jammed back to back against Vargaard. I cannot even see him. He could disappear and I would not know.

"Step with me," his voice commands. *"Pivot left. Yes, that's right, now slide to the left. Just like that. Now pivot again. Now! Now!"*

I listen to his commands, calmly executing them, feeling the whistle of blades that nearly touch me but don't, feeling the burning energy of the other two Nakuraki spinning upward.

Jendaya grunts between her teeth. "If you're trying to get to your father, don't think I won't beat you to him. It will be fun, though, to see how he chooses. Will he choose the heart of a faithless daughter or that of a devout Queen? I think I know. They don't call him Admiral Redtide for nothing. He will stain the seas red for me."

"He will not," I gasp.

"Don't listen to her," Vargaard gasps and I realize, with a quick glance at him, that he's wearing out. He must not have healed in his time away from me — in fact, he looks worse than he did before he left. My heart stutters in my chest.

"Oh, definitely listen," Haszinth whispers as he lunges. His spirit blade connects, ripping a slice from Vargaard's leg.

Jendaya laughs as I pivot, dancing away from her. She got too close, reaching with her free hand toward the Tranquility Sword. With her Nakuraki free, it does not hide me from her.

"Already I have sent my Farrakki before me to claim his fleet as my prize and ransack his ships," Jendaya tells me. "They will create a ship of spirit and souls and set out across this Sea of Souls with him as my captain and me as the queen not only of the mortal worlds but of all worlds."

"Ambitious," I say through my teeth, but as I spin I must duck under the sword of this female Nakuraki. Her eyes glitter and her spirit hand ghosts through my hair, unable to snatch it. "But unlikely. He will never serve you."

Jendaya's smile turns cruel. Her favorite kind. "Ah, Ilsaletta. What a thing to say. A little ignorant, don't you think? You see, he already does."

"Don't listen, my sun, my stars. Do not give her such power over you. "

I think Vargaard wants to pause with me. I see how his expression ripples and rips and is remade in variations of concern.

"You are not her plaything. You are Ilsaletta Redtide, brave and sure."

But already I am halting in my tracks, all my doubts swarming up to fill me, to snatch from me any ability to know what to do in this moment. I can't see the clear path. I can't ...

"Ilsaletta! You've been touched!"

I look down. My tunic is slashed with blood. I look up again, sharing a breath of horror with Vargaard, but then he grunts, as Haszinth's blade barely misses him and he's forced to turn from me to keep his bade deflecting that greater Nakuraki's blows.

I cannot follow his movements any more than that. My vision is filled with the female Nakuraki. She spins, a blade in her hand — a blade I had not seen before. It's no longer than her palm. As she spins her hands make complicated patterns ,and though I lift both my swords up, I know it is too late. I am not quick enough, not fast enough. I barely catch a panicked cry from Vargaard as his spirit ripples.

I grit my teeth, heart racing.

And then she's gone, torn like a shred of mist in a sudden breeze, lifted up into the air and dissipated.

"Ilsaletta!" Vargaard cries.

There's a terrible scream — one I don't recognize.

Something clamps around my waist, squeezing out my breath and filling me with flashes of pain. My face is pressed into leather and cloth as I'm snatched up from the ground.

I've made a terrible mistake, a fatal error and now I will pay. I am captured.

I draw in a breath, ready to say my goodbyes to Vargaard. But my breath catches in my throat as I hear the mourning cry from above me.

"*Mercy!*" Shrieks the spirit bird.

I twist my head hard and look up to see a grim-faced Stekkan. He is leaning out from his horse as only a rider as expert as he can manage, and he looks almost as if he is in an exhibition as he holds a sword by the blade — ow! — in one hand, and has me gripped roughly, and not very certainly at all, in the other.

He lets out a shuddering fear-laced whine and I wriggle to help him fling me belly-down on his mount.

"*Sheathe the Mercy Sword,*" Vargaard barks.

Behind us, Jendaya's curse splits the air. That blasted horn is still sounding for reinforcements.

I try, but the horse is moving and my hands are full. It's a full breath before Stekkan prizes the Tranquility Sword from my hand. He keeps his palm pressed to the hilt and I grip the Mercy Sword as I pull myself around him to take a more stable seat riding pillion. It's only now that I see we are still riding as fast as possible in the thick forest and our horse is rolling his eyes and favoring one foot.

I steal a glance over one shoulder and catch a last look at the melee we are fleeing. Jendaya is still mounted, her horse rearing, mouth open in a furious snarl. At her feet, head smashed and broken, is the count who owned the Nakuraki sword that surely has sliced Stekkan's hand to ribbons. There's movement all around, but I can't register who else has survived, before the foliage covers them from view.

"That could have gone better," Stekkan gasps.

"*It could also have gone much worse,*" Vargaard says and his deep baritone is wary. "*Were you set upon suddenly … by the princess? The odds are so narrow.*"

"This is the last time I help you try for spontaneous revenge," I hiss at Stekkan, feeling my face grow hot at what Vargaard surely hears as a confession.

I do not want to confess that we saw an opportunity and took it.

He sighs within my mind.

"If he's scolding you, tell him that it's his fault for staying away for so long that we thought he was dead," Stekkan whispers.

"*I am not dead.*"

"If he's telling you that he's not dead, then tell him he should show up when things get hairy or this is how it goes."

Stekkan, it seems, has grown a spine.

"*At the exact wrong time and he's using it to stand against his only capable ally.*"

"I'm capable. Sort of."

Stekkan snorts.

"*Not enough to attack a princess,*" Vargaard tells me. "*Wait for me next time.*"

I was waiting. But I did not know if he would come, or if he had done as I wished and returned to the Fisher King.

"*Know this, hope of my hopes. If I do not come for you, it is because I cannot. Never will I choose to turn my back on you.*"

"Are you capable enough to flee into the woods?" Stekkan gasps, breaking into our sweet moment.

"The Duke handles you too familiarly."

Something crashes behind us and keeps on crashing. They're hunting us. And they are very close.

He's a king now, I remind Vargaard, but aloud I say. "I think we can flee capably, Stekkan."

Vargaard grunts as if he's not sure of that. *"We must do all we can to make you mistress of flight and queen of retreat."*

"Vargaard?"

"Yes?"

"Is that your breath I feel on my neck?" I pause. "Vargaard?"

He does not answer. And perhaps that is for the best.

CHAPTER TEN
NAKURAKI

I must tell her, I think.

That I have chosen her.

That my power fades because my attachment is now to her and not to the world of the shadow.

That I lose the memories she needs and the wisdom we require.

That I am becoming none of the things she needs.

That I am not just mortal with her, but becoming more vulnerable yet.

CHAPTER ELEVEN

"Don't breathe so loudly," Stekkan whispers in my ear.

I try to slow my breathing but it only makes it worse and I nearly choke.

"Do not listen to the popinjay." Vargaard is on edge.

He does not like how heavily we have been relying on the Tranquility Sword to mask us as we weave through the forest to the river. I do not know if it is the situation — surely the occasional scream or crash would set anyone on edge — or if it is the reliance on a magic that is not his.

"I do not like to see you in situations of such danger. You are a looking glass, not a cudgel and should not be used for what you were not made."

I smirk inwardly. He has made me a monster hunter. How else did he see this going? Obviously, if I am to hunt monsters, then I will be in danger.

"No one still living sees you so. Not even the jumped-up king — now that he knows about me."

I peer sidelong at Stekkan. We both stand with breath

mingled in the hollow of a tree, clutching the pommel of the Tranquility Sword together. We lost the horse early on. His foot was too twisted to walk. We kept what we could and carried on with the second horse. We must ride double or we will not be invisible to the eye.

"*Mercy,*" Stekkan's macaw hoots quietly. She's looking at what he is fixed upon — dark figures weaving between the trees, searching.

They are why we shelter in this hollow tree. They've grown so thick on the ground that it is becoming impossible to ride the horse without half-tripping over them. It is — I think — every husk they made in Swordheart, marching out from that city in these bloated hunting parties, looking like the monsters they are with their faces and heads split open and coronas of brightly colored smoke ever bubbling out from their ruined faces. Some of them ride on strange monsters — creatures with four heads or nine lashing tails. The Farrakki. I do not know how many of them Jendaya unleashed from that rip between the dead and the living, but I have seen three today. If I have seen three as I run and flee, how many more must there be out there?

We have made it within sight of the river. It slinks along its bed between the waving rushes, slow and miserable as if it, too, is ill with all that has happened. I wish I had the luxury to stand on the bank and sit in peace with the flowing water, maybe let it carry me far away from all of this, but where would we go? I must think and think hard on what we can do.

"*You are not a god,*" Vargaard tells me fiercely as if I do not know it. *"You do not know it — clearly — or you would stop taking all of this terrible assault on humanity on your narrow shoulders as if you are responsible for it."*

With Stekkan and I wedged between moss and moldering wood, the smell of crushed mushrooms in our noses, Vargaard is forced to press in close, too. I cannot even see him in this cramped space, but I feel him flickering, just as I keep catching tiny hints of Mercy stalking up and down Stekkan's shoulders.

What else would I do *but* take this on my shoulders? There is nowhere to run from it. No other option but to tackle it head-on.

"You are one woman, not an army."

Is that what he learned in the Seas of Shadows when he was gone so long?

I don't expect an answer. He is cryptic about these things. I am surprised when he chooses to speak.

"It is exactly what I learned, Ilsaletta. They are together in that great sea — one knot of souls working in tandem. And they beat me until I was just one more broken soul trampled under the feet of the sea."

I feel the air in my lungs freeze. I dare not let him do anything like that ever again.

"Let? I am your servant in all things, my heart is yours from the dawn to the dusk of life, but Ilsaletta, you do not let *me do anything. I give of my free will. I give of what little is left to me. Why should I not be generous? And though you are my sun, would you deny me this?"*

I feel properly chastened. My cheeks glow brightly.

"But now we know they cannot be destroyed from within

and they must *be either collected or destroyed. If Jendaya has them together, too, what can stop her?"*

I agree with that.

"But don't forget — for us, this has always been about the personal. About what is right here in front of our faces. We can do as much as we can, but we cannot do everything. We are not birds in the sky who see all. We are not queens and kings who send and command."

Well, Stekkan is. I shoot a glance at him and see his jaw is clenched and his face pale. Perhaps, he wrestles demons of his own.

"I am no demon."

I barely manage not to laugh at that. I had not meant him. I mean the crushing guilt that I cannot be more.

"Keep putting one foot in front of the other. One step at a time. That is all we can be. The ones who deal with the problem before us and the next and the next."

But what about the big problems? The overarching ones that affect all of our lives?

"If everyone were to tackle just those problems right in front of them and do it well, then those would be solved as well."

Wise, perhaps, in a time when there were more people alive who cared about the good. Instead, there are only we few tiny remnants.

"And yet, in the end, that's how it always is. A few good people clinging to what is right while the rest thunder head-long towards shallow destruction."

I swallow. I am overwhelmed by it all. The book digs into my back. Stekkan has strapped it there. The slash across my chest is healing, but it stings badly though the Mercy Sword helps it heal. It takes all of Vargaard's talk to keep me from slipping away into the heavy tranquility that wants to descend with both swords in my grasp.

A sudden sound makes my breath hitch in my lungs before I realize with wry amusement that it is only Stekkan. He's managed to fall asleep standing up within this tree, his body pressed in the hollow of it, face pillowed against a clump of green moss. Perhaps, in the end, all I'll be able to do is save us two.

"And is that so bad?"

I am silent. It is certainly so bad. That I have failed so utterly so far haunts me. I cannot listen to the screams I have not prevented. And when I think that perhaps Stekkan and I will be the only living breathing humans to escape this with our lives remaining and our souls untainted, it makes something in me lurch.

"I must confess something." Vargaard's mental voice is tight. It arrests me.

There is no need for him to confess anything.

"I've kept it far too long from you."

He moves and now I can see him just barely in the hollow of the tree, nestled into my shadow.

Cold rushes over me and I swallow, tense as footsteps draw closer. Someone is peering into every hollow and hillock. Small animals chitter at him and birds fly up in squawking horror at this disruption of natural things.

"My Ilsaletta. My heart."

Vargaard sounds like he is choking over his own mental

voice. I clench my jaw and ready myself to weather whatever storm he will unleash.

A twig snaps nearby.

"I was born again when I was born in your shadow," my guardian says. *"You know this. But what you don't know — what I did not realize — is that in making that choice, I have lost what came before."*

What does that mean?

He seems distraught as he answers me. *"I have lost the other Vargaards. Their memories flee me. They flap like tattered flags and I do not know what is lost from their ragged edges, only that they grow thinner and sparser every day. Whatever help I can give you is diminishing. Fading. "*

If I thought I was chilled before I am frigid inside now. I didn't realize how much I was counting his added knowledge as certain.

Can he get them back?

"I cannot. They are gone forever."

Is he devastated by their loss? Has he lost ... himself?

He bites his shadow lip. *"I fear I have disappointed you."*

Never that.

I fear that in choosing you, I have crippled your chances.

I am too honest to dismiss that. He probably has. And yet ...

I had felt his breath on my neck. I cling to the feeling of it. So much so, that I almost think I can feel it gusting across my skin again, soft and warm and *near.* I shiver very slightly with the delight of it.

"You do feel it."

I suck in a gasp of surprise. And I can't help how my fists clench with longing. Does this mean ... can it possibly mean ...

His eyes are wild as his words come out like a confession. "I am being made flesh."

But how?

He shakes his head, shadows scattering.

"I do not know. I did not anticipate this. And I fear ... my darling Ilsaletta, I fear that if I am made flesh then I will no longer be the dark magic you need to keep you safe."

But he'd ... he'd be with me? The thought makes my eyes prick with sudden tears and my breath hitch. I close my eyes for a moment and draw in a breath.

I could touch him? Hold him?

I could swear that I feel the barest ghost of a kiss on my cheek as I think those words. I want this. More than I can possibly confess. I want to wrap him up in my embrace and press my lips all over him.

"I'd be too vulnerable to be what you need."

On the contrary, he will be *exactly* what I need. The possibility is too big. I am choking on it, overwhelmed by a hope I don't dare claim.

"I will be your shadow for as long as I can, until the last shred of magic is ripped away and I am nothing but a man."

Nothing but a man. He says it so wistfully, while to me it is the precise longing of my heart. My hand on the Tranquility Sword trembles and I huff in a long, aching breath.

"Don't leave me, my heart," I whisper to Vargaard. Will he go when he is fully free? Will I lose him?

"Never will I leave you. Never will I abandon you."

I almost sigh my relief but the sigh is arrested while still in my throat at another whisper.

"What do we have here?"

I turn my head in slow horror. Peeking into our tree is a husk of a man, a purple monster rising up from his broken face. To my utter horror, both halves of his slack mouth suddenly curl into a bifurcated smile, showing red-stained teeth and he laughs as the purple cloud bubbles hot and fast, building over him.

I clench the Tranquility Sword, willing myself not to scream, but before I even can, Vargaard darts out and with a deft twist of his hands, he snaps the man's neck and throws him to the side, and then still huffing with the effort, he spins and his eyes meet mine in a mix of guilt and longing as he mouths the word, "*Run.*"

I shake Stekkan awake with a hand clamped over his mouth.

"*Oh, how the mighty have fallen!*" Mercy hoots.

But I pay her no mind as I push Stekkan out of the tree, and together we grasp the Tranquility Sword and run toward the yawning river.

CHAPTER TWELVE

"If this is your father's riverboat then we are exactly where we need to be." Stekkan is the only person who can make having slept in hollow trees and eating stale bread between running sprints look like a prelude to a grand social occasion. He shed his bright silk jacket when we found an overturned coach that just happened to have clothing that fit a country gentleman. He's now dressed in a close olive jacket, tan breeches, and knee-high, brown, leather boots with turned-down cuffs. He so outfitted himself with knives and even a small axe that he almost has *me* fooled into believing he can use them.

He's been … not Stekkan this past day. He has followed me timidly, sleeping as much as possible. Even when he dressed he did it quietly without checking himself in whatever gleaming surface was near or even inspecting the cut of his jacket before slipping it on.

I am dressed in what we found, too. The other

gentleman must have been a young man, still not fully grown, for his slender-cut jacket fits me perfectly under my father's ship's coat. I'm just grateful for clean, warm clothing and no skirts. We found no bodies among the ruined trunks and destroyed carriage. No horses, either, so perhaps the two of them went on foot.

Or perhaps they are among those hunting us now.

It is the second day of playing hound and rabbit. My injuries are healed, thanks to the Mercy Sword. Stekkan and I still cling to the Tranquility Sword together. We have not had the time or leisure to investigate the sword he stole, though doubtless the resonance with it contributes to the other two swords we hold. We have collected three of seven. I should be delighted by this. Instead, I am worried. These three have nearly cost us everything.

Whatever Nakuraki lies within will be subject to you, Vargaard assured me as we fled, unsure why I hesitated. *And that will be one less of my brethren who can harm you.*

But physical needs trumped curiosity as we scrambled from tree to bush and from bush to sheltering rock. The sheer numbers flooding past us tied my belly into knots. I would not be the first to reach my father's ship. This was certain, no matter where he had washed up along the river. And I was worried. Though we were on foot and forced from the main roads, we were still covering a lot of ground. I would have thought to see him much sooner.

Now, however, all the hairs on my arms and neck stand up as I study the shore of the river, chewing my lip. It's the gloaming and the banks are wreathed in mist, but not so wreathed that we do not see four riverboats linked together, lights strung from bow to stern, and loud with sounds that seem jubilant, though it can be hard to tell whether those on board revel in triumph or maliciousness.

Where they found so many small boats to ferry people back and forth remains a mystery to me, but the river is thick with them, and laced with shouts and hails as the boats pass one another.

I cannot tell what has happened here or who controls these boats. It is the enemy on the small boats, but whether they meet the riverboats to treat for peace, or whether they have overwhelmed them already, I do not know.

I shift my stance.

"Investigate the sword," Vargaard urges. *"We may, perhaps, need it."*

But I can only wield one sword at a time. Even clinging to a second to give me invisibility is causing me difficulty. Two people attached constantly by the need to hold a sword between them soon grow weary of one another. Stekkan and I are testy already.

Besides, if I can only use one sword, then I want it to be the Mercy Sword

"You do not need to be attached to the Mercy Sword," Vargaard says.

Perhaps he is growing weary of me, too.

"I am not weary of you, but I am your protector. I will guard against the enemy more than any sword can."

If I could, I would cast all three swords within a furnace and melt them to slag.

"I do not believe that you can melt down one of these swords and dismiss the Nakuraki. I think you would end up with a chunk of melted slag that still held the spirit. Either we collect them all and see if together they can bring down your rival, or we dispose of their Nakuraki some other way."

We could find out but for that, I will need to study the book.

"Or."

Or I could investigate the sword. I frown at it and then wipe my hands on my skirts. I am not ready. But I'm also not ready to leap aboard a boat, ferry myself between similar crafts decked high with the enemy, and announce myself blindly to whoever captains that riverboat flotilla, so this seems like the lesser of the two.

"Are you considering drawing the new sword?" Stekkan whispers.

"Yes," I whisper back as I draw out the new sword from my belt, wrappings and all. It did not respond to Stekkan when he grabbed it from the ground, nor has it so much as flickered when its hilt has been brushed — not like the Spirit Sword Jendaya wields. Poor Stekkan. He'd had to let me stitch his hand for him. It was still a mess and he refused to take the Mercy Sword to heal it.

"Give it to me," he hisses. "I'll try it."

"He absolutely should not be the one to try it."

I look at Stekkan questioning. "I did not know you were keen on swords."

"I am not in the slightest keen," he says, and his pout is too pretty to take seriously. He strikes a pose to emphasize his next words. Did this kind of thing help him in court? "But I am king now, and with that comes responsibility."

Vargaard's swirling form is silent. Does he have nothing to say to that?

"How can I argue with responsibility?"

"Besides," Stekkan says, eyeing Vargaard warily. He still is not comfortable around my shadow friend. "If it possesses me or otherwise draws me in, you will be able to cut me down ... before ... before I lose my soul or whatever."

"*Whatever,*" Mercy repeats mournfully.

I feel my jaw drop. "You'd take that risk?"

"His thinking has great merit. I accept this plan."

"I don't accept this plan," I say, shocked.

Stekkan gives me a reproving look, setting one finger over his lips to remind me to be silent here in the reeds along the river bank. They wave wildly, as distressed as I am. Only their fecund scent keeps me grounded. This is madness.

"I am your king, Ilsaletta," Stekkan says uneasily, running a hand through his black hair as if he wishes he were not saying this, and yet pressing on. "And I order you to relinquish my prize."

"You order me?" I say, but it's not offense that motivates my words. It's surprise.

"I've been out of sorts," he tells me, leaning in confidentially. I think his cheeks are flushed. It's hard to tell in the half-light. "I've lost ... well, you've seen how we scurry like hunted rabbits. It would get to any man. I need this."

"Oh. Ohhh." Vargaard is cryptic.

"Do you have something to add to this discussion?" I ask him calmly.

Stekkan's eyes go wide as he turns to Vargaard. "Is he saying something?"

"*It took his confidence away,*" Vargaard says. "*What sword might do that?*"

I exhale a breath remembering the list I read in the library.

"The Tenacity Sword," I say thoughtfully, glancing at Stekkan. "It stole your confidence when it cut your hand."

He sucks in a long breath and his eyes widen and then he nods decisively. "Well then. Let's get it back."

"Are you sure?" I say, placing the Tenacity Sword on the ground between us. We're all squatting down together, Vargaard, Stekkan, and I. Even Mercy has hopped off Stekkan's shoulder and is crouched beside him, staring at the gleaming sword with the double cross guard.

It's Stekkan who answers. "I'm not ready. Not for any of this. I just want to find your father and hand this responsibility over to him."

"That's the lack of confidence talking," I say, but I'm not certain. His shared secret has made something twinge in me. Is this why I am so intent on finding my father? Do I also believe he will save us all and that I could put down this terrible burden? Perhaps. Perhaps, I am just that much of a fool.

"*You are no fool.*"

I swallow. "We already have two swords, Stekkan. We could just throw this one away. Deep into the water or into the furnace of a forge. Destroy it."

"You know you can't do that. These swords are a key one way or another."

Stekkan's words overlap with Vargaard's as he also says. "We both know that we can't do that. What's lost can be retrieved and if it were easy to destroy these swords someone would have done it already."

That, I'm not so certain of. Power is a tempting thing. It draws the weakest and worst like moths to a flame. What they cannot earn with skill and discipline, they take by force from others.

"Wise words, my Vali."

Stekkan takes a last fortifying breath and then he reaches forward and draws the sword smoothly from its wrappings, standing to brandish it before him. We all come to our feet with him, our attention focused together on the sword. I think my hands are shaking as they grip the Mercy Sword and Tranquility Sword both.

We do not have to wait. The Nakuraki's leap is sudden. One moment there is nothing, the next, she is there, a sword in her hand, and violence in her eyes. She spins, eyeing me, Vargaard, and Stekkan. The moment she sees that Stekkan grips her sword, she falls to both knees, head bent, arms crossed over her chest.

Stekkan and I share a sickly look over her shadowy head. It's hard to make out her distinct features in the darkness, but she flickers just like Vargaard, moving from a woman in long robes, to one in close-fitting fighting clothing, to one in a long wrapping dress, then back to the robes. Her hair changes length and dress, just as his did. But then, suddenly, unlike him — she settles. And her clothing matches Stekkan's, her hair is dressed in a ragged braid like my own, and when she speaks I cannot hear her voice, though Stekkan's face grows stony and grim.

"She says she lives to serve," Stekkan says wryly. "Don't we all?"

CHAPTER THIRTEEN

Stekkan with the Tenacity Sword is a terrible thing. He holds his head high and his eyes are suddenly sharp as knife edges.

"I have a plan. Nakuraki. Ilsaletta."

He seems to almost glow. I exchange looks with Vargaard who offers a faint shrug as Mercy flutters up and lands on top of Stekkan's head. She holds her beak high, looking imperious.

"We will take one of those boats and float right into the thick of the flotilla and I will demand to see Admiral Redtide — as his king."

Stekkan lifts his chin high, too, matching Mercy as he strikes a noble pose. If he wasn't so beautiful, he would look ridiculous.

I'm gaping now.

I hardly manage to spit out, "And if your wife is there?"

"Then we will ... reunite. Her, with her army of corricles and husks at her back, and me with my Monster Hunter at mine."

"*No. This is insane.*" Vargaard's shadow form is agitated, pacing back and forth and flickering. "*Responsibility, I like. Throwing ourselves into the maw of the beast? Not so much.*"

I stare at him, frowning as he paces. I'm caught by how his clothing does not change. It reflects Stekkan's current mode of dress, only it fits a little better. When was the last time it changed? Is it ... staying the same?

I feel slightly ill at the thought. If he is frozen in one mode of dress, then this proves his claim that he is becoming a flesh-and-blood man. How long will it take for him to completely transform? Were we alone and in peace, I'd be filled with anticipation. As it is — I am deeply troubled. If Stekkan walks us into the middle of our enemies and Vargaard becomes a real man there, we will be terribly vulnerable. Time is short.

"*Terribly short. We must act one way or another — or flee.*"

"You want the pair of us to walk right into the midst of hundreds of enemies as visible, easy targets," I ask. I feel my expression flickering as I try to sift between so many thoughts and emotions.

Stekkan is nodding energetically. I have never seen this Stekkan. This wild, intent, outrageously courageous Stekkan. It feels like watching a puppy turn into a wolf before your eyes.

His words are precise, his whole attitude changed. "We are outnumbered. We have no special weapon or great magic. Our last chance to turn the tides is somewhere on that boat. Either your father — the Admiral — is still on our side and requires our guidance to deliver this land, or he is hopelessly enmeshed in the plans of our enemies and our hope in him is lost, in which case we must do what the small always do to win against the great."

"And what is that?" I ask carefully, as Vargaard makes a terrible, disbelieving face.

"Maybe it isn't the Tenacity Sword. Was there an Insanity Sword on your list? A sword of Foolhardiness? A sword of Arrogant Disaster?"

None of those, I assure him.

"We act ... insane," Stekkan says mildly as his Nakuraki nods along from her place of supplication.

Perhaps I was wrong.

"Well, you've planned well for that," I say dryly.

"Preserve us." Vargaard's words sound like a curse.

"They will be so thrown off that they will not know how to respond, and that will give us an opening." Stekkan is nothing but determined.

"An opening to do what?" I find myself asking, my mouth dry.

"To be creative."

"No." Vargaard makes a chopping motion with his hand.

"To find a chink in their armor," Stekkan presses as his spirit bird paces across his shoulders and then back again.

"No."

"And you'll just stride in there?" I don't want to sound disbelieving, but it still slips into my voice. "To where

Jendaya and representatives of half the nations of the world are likely waiting?"

His face softens slightly, frowns. "You won't? Take a risk and go when it might mean the life of your father one way or another?"

He has shut my mouth effectively with that argument. I cannot find another objection to voice.

"Trust me. I can. I am all for bold plans — but only ones likely to work. Let us stop and consider other options."

"And if we fail?" I ask, feeling a chill wash over me.

"Then we die," Stekkan says grimly, his lovely full lips forming a grim line. "And so does all the world."

I stare at him. Where has this Stekkan come from?

"This does not sound like you," I say carefully.

He draws in a long breath and pulls a silky handker-chief from his pocket to mop his brow. Better.

"I have looked into my own heart and seen what is there."

"If you say so."

"I did not like the view," Stekkan says, looking away, slightly flushed.

"Anyone can be attracted to a monster," I say, trying to comfort him, but it does not help. If anything, his cheeks are brighter yet.

"I have decided that if you can be a monster hunter simply because you have a shadow protecting you, then why can I not do the same?"

I glance at Vargaard. To my surprise, he has paused, looking thoughtful.

"Your shadow warrior is listening," Stekkan says,

pointing at Vargaard. "He knows I am right. If there are only two of us, then why would we not multiply it to four?"

This is Stekkan? Stekkan who hid behind my skirts only days ago? I am worried that his confidence will only last until we first face an enemy.

"Always a worry with new warriors."

I am even more afraid that with his dramatic personality, he might throw himself too far into this part to the other side — from nervous hiding to bold dares that cannot pay off.

"Another legitimate worry to have."

But then again, he's not wrong. If we do not meet my father, the chances of finding an ally are grim. Besides which, the thought of him being held or hurt by the enemy makes me ill. I wish I knew what was happening on those riverboats. I wish there was any way at all to find out before committing to a course of action but the moving boats on the water make sneaking in there nearly impossible. Stekkan is not wrong. The only way that has any hope is to either go in fighting from the first moment, or to go in with ridiculous boldness and demand to be seen.

"I see your concern on your face," Stekkan says to me. "But this is not one of your books of history. You cannot know ahead of time how the story goes. We are only two. We have no eyes and ears spread out to report to us. No subjects to command. No friends to ally with. We can only do the best we can from our limited, close perspective."

"I don't even understand the magic we're dealing with," I whisper my confession, glancing over my shoulder as if I am being eavesdropped on. "The Sea of Souls, the swords, the gem. I see them work but I don't understand what fuels such magic or how to turn it back."

"You are not a god," he shrugs. "Nor am I, though I am king."

"Stekkan finally speaks sense. It is not for you to sort the end from the beginning. And we've already seen I cannot fight this battle alone on the other plane. I would prefer a better plan. But perhaps he is right. Perhaps this is the moment we should seize."

Vargaard seems uncomfortable admitting this. His discomfort makes my own stomach roll and heave. But what else will we do? Flee into the darkness? Hope to find a place of refuge far across the sea? Attempt — with no way to know where Jendaya has sent them — to find one of the other swords to steal?

"Then I suppose your plan is the only one that makes sense," I tell Stekkan.

"We could still run," he says, looking over *his* shoulder now.

"We could never have run," I say sadly. "Not to anywhere safe."

"We will make our own safe place. I will make one here for you within my heart."

"Then let's go show them the king of Cragspear," Stekkan says, gesturing to his Nakuraki to stand. "Do you have a name?"

If she answers him, I do not hear her voice.

"Then I will give you the name Penitence to go with my bird, Mercy."

"That's the worst name." I think Vargaard is hiding a smirk.

"Guard my front, Penitence," Stekkan commands, and then his tone changes to a more courtly Stekkan-like tone. "And if you don't mind, Monster Hunter, you shall guard the rear."

"I live to serve," I say dryly as Vargaard lifts an eyebrow at me.

"Mercy! Mercy!" His bird scolds and she keeps on scolding as we stride out from under cover and toward the nearest boat.

CHAPTER FOURTEEN

I don't know what I expect from an evil army of former humans. Organization, perhaps.

I do not find it. What we find on the dark beach — busy enough with comings and goings to disguise a few more people with ease — is a corricle picking his nails. He glances up at us in alarm. His small craft has a lit lantern on a pole in the front and two rowers at the ready. They sit unhappily at the oars, their eyes darting in every direction and their ruined faces ghastly as smoke continues to gush up from what was once their heads. The corricle will not look at them directly.

"What do you want?"

"To board the ships," Stekkan says shortly.

The corricle's eyes focus on the blade in Stekkan's hand. He was a boy of maybe eighteen before the reddish-colored squirrel he produces revealed his black tattered heart. He looks from the blade to me and his eyes are dull holes.

"No passengers. Show your avatar or surrender to death."

Stekkan waves off this demand as if it is an offer, his lip curling and his hand making a flicking motion.

"I am King of Cragspear. Take me to the boats."

The corricle laughs a nasty, derision-thick laugh and I sigh because I know what comes next. I will have to fight him and his red squirrel.

"*We,*" Vargaard reminds me reprovingly but while I'm still drawing the Mercy Sword and Vargaard is leaping forward. He's right.

Stekken shocks me by awkwardly lifting his own blade. It glints in the moonlight, and before he can say a word, his Nakuraki slides forward to the very edge of the sword's shadow, twists herself, and plunges her spirit sword through the corricle's neck.

He dies, still gurgling, as I hurry forward so that Vargaard can rip one of the husks from the boat and plunge him beneath the dark water. The dying husk's smoke is bubbles at first, which burst along the top of the water, the colorful smoke puffing from the popped bubbles is whipped away by the wind and then there is nothing at all.

My mouth has fallen open by the time I realize that Stekkan is lashing the second husk to his own oars. Penitence holds her shadow blade to the throat of the creature and makes tiny little violent flicks so he feels the edge of it. His tearing gasps are not enough to wring my heart. Not anymore. These have chosen their side.

"Now you understand how it feels, Ilsaletta," Stekkan

says coolly, though his face is green and wobbling slightly. "It's not very enjoyable watching other people create violent chaos, is it?"

"No," I say in horrified wonder. It is not enjoyable at all.

I wade through the blood-churned waters and thrust the boat out into the waves, leaping in at the last second.

"Row, husk," Stekkan says in a hollow voice, taking up a place in the stern where he can work the tiller with skilled hands. His bird hugs in tight to his ear, cursing under her breath as she stretches her wings and totters back and forth. "Guard the bow, monster hunter."

My words come out slowly, heavy with shock. "As you say, my king."

"This is unexpected."

"The most unexpected," I agree with Varhaard checking my swords. The Tranquility Sword is still in place. I shift the Mercy Sword in my grip, unwilling to sheathe it.

"Unexpected is a good quality in a king," Stekkan says lightly but his voice is still laced with something that sounds like bitterness.

"I don't know where you got that idea," I disagree, my voice thick with horror.

"Likely from his queen." Vargaard's mental voice is wry. *"I can't decide if I think this plan is madness or a stroke of genius."*

Coming from Vargaard, that is almost a ringing endorsement.

I had expected opposition even as we rowed, but to my surprise, the other craft skimming over the water pay us little mind. Perhaps all they see is a pair of passengers and the husk rowing us, making himself known quite clearly with his sickly yellow smoke. We are far enough away from them that I cannot catch the details of their looks or conversations, and they cannot catch ours.

"Steady now," Stekkan warns us. "Steady as she goes."

I think that perhaps he is talking to himself. I still can't believe he's doing this.

"He'd better not drop the Tenacity Sword or he might not realize how he's doing it, either."

I keep my grip on my sword firm. My belly rolls miserably as the high riverboat sides loom ahead, dark with pitch, rolling with the flow of the river, and alight with lanterns. The buzz of voices and clatter of metal on metal could be eating. I will hope that is what it is. I will hope that these corricles are turned back by my father's guards and that is why they swarm the waters below. My hope is as faint as the moonlight from behind the gathering clouds.

Someone laughs uproariously, but from here, we cannot see anyone aboard. We are already in the boat's shadow, skimming up to where a bell hangs from her railing. I am conscious of how the lantern on the bow shifts our shadows — how we have little help from the veiled moon.

Stekkan doesn't ring the bell to alert the people above when we draw in to where a rope ladder hangs down. I'm surprised there is no watcher waiting for boats. It seems like a terrible lapse.

"It is bad form. They must feel very confident. Or their watcher is dead. I do not like this."

Neither alternative makes me feel better. My stomach swims with nerves.

Stekkan signals to me to be silent, jams a cloth in the husk's mouth — is that his silken handkerchief? —and then, sword still in one hand, he begins to climb up the rope ladder, the shadow of his Nakuraki streaming before him, his Mercy bird flying circles over his head.

"This is madness," I breathe.

But in my mind, Vargaard is laughing.

"Why should he not make a bold move? I've been complaining all this time that he wouldn't step up. I can hardly complain now when he does."

I think this is a bad idea. The only thing that makes me press on is the sure knowledge that my father is up there. I grab the bottom rungs of the ladder.

"Kick your boat away. You don't want to leave something close by to alert anyone that you are here and that bound rower will make a sound if he can."

I kick free of the boat and kick it away in one motion. Unlike Stekkan, I climb with both swords sheathed. This swaying rope ladder feels uncertain at best.

"This is the best bad idea that your king has had other than raising you from the dead and carrying you out of Swordheart in his necklace. I make no bones about it, Ilsaletta. I am only here for you. I care not whether your king falls in battle aboard that ship or succeeds in gaining an ally and taking back his kingdom. I care not whether your father lives or perishes. I care only for you. If you live, I live. If you die, all is lost."

Even now when you know I'm only a woman and not the goddess you thought when you were reborn?

"Especially now. What need has a goddess of me? But as a woman? Perhaps you need me after all."

I do need him.

He seems pleased at that, so I climb on, heart in my throat. I do not like this. But I do like who I am with.

Stekkan disappears over the rail above far too quickly. Perhaps his Nakuraki is advising him, also. But there is no scream or shout of challenge. There is no sign of him being thrown back the way he came.

I will take that as a victory for now.

"Get ready. It's about to start. Brace yourself for anything."

The last rung is slippery in my hand, despite being good jute. I take a deep breath, brace myself for whatever mystery lies beyond, and pull myself up and over the rail.

CHAPTER FIFTEEN

The flotilla of riverboats is lashed together side by side so that the party we are joining can move from boat to boat freely. So secure are they that no enemy lurks in the waters surrounding them, that they have posted no guard. And no wonder. We saw no one who might challenge them other than ourselves.

By luck or fate, the boat we've climbed aboard hosts the head table for this particular party. Beyond it, I can see the figures on the decks of the other boats dining and drinking and laughing. Is that a knife-throwing contest?

And an axe-throwing competition, two wrestling bouts, and some duel I do not recognize regarding corricles. It seems that today. evil feasts.

Isn't that every day, though?

These people are in high spirits — and high color. Boiling bright smoke appears here and there in their midst and glowing creatures circle some of them or charge into the fray of a battle of skill or strength.

Well then. They are not a ship of the good. Not anymore. I don't know why I was clinging to that notion. But not all present show signs of turning. Perhaps — could it be that my father negotiates but is not turned?

I ease the Mercy Sword slowly from its sheath.

I can only look past the main tableau for so long. I have to face what is right in front of us, and once my sword is free, I do, rolling my shoulders and stretching my neck as if I, and not Vargaard, will deal with this next thing.

"I will need every shred of strength and skill you possess," he assures me. *"I am only so swift and sure as the shadow I dwell in."*

Before us is spread a long table, ringed with a mix of sailors and soldiers. And facing each other over the oaken surface are Queen Jendaya and my father.

"Don't make a sound."

I have not made one yet, but my breath is caught in my lungs. So is Stekkan's from where he waits in the shadows just ahead of me.

Admiral Redtide — my father — seems unharmed. With his uniform starched and ironed and well-fitted, his feathered hat on his head, and maps spread before him, he could be back in his library at our home. I can almost smell the peppermint in his pockets. There is no sign of smoke or smoke creatures around him. Not even a whiff of one. I lean forward, trying to be sure I'm not missing something.

Don't move. Don't even breathe.

But Stekkan is moving and breathing, already stepping forward with a slight sway as if he is at a ball choosing a partner, rather than facing down his enemy and mine. And I have promised to back his play.

Vargaard curses rather colorfully but I ignore him. He was the one who said this might be genius.

Curses or no curses, I can hardly leave my fresh-minted king to face this alone. And I can't help the hope welling up in me. My father facing the queen. My father with no sign of the plague having turned him and not yet dead. My heart is in my throat with the certainty that he will negotiate peace for us now. We will not need to hunt down swords or destroy them. We will not need to flee into the countryside and likely die with the rest. A hero is here and for once, it doesn't have to be me pretending while Vargaard does all the work.

"You have been as much of a hero as I, Ilsaletta. Stop selling yourself short. But back to this. You know your father better than I. Is he … he has not turned?"

I study my father's face and posture as I hurry to take a place at Stekkan's back. My father's broad shoulders and hoary eyebrows are easily visible, his face freshly shaven as always, hair neatly tied back and eyes blazing. The tiny smile playing around the edges of his mouth is him. Certainly. But he hasn't noticed me yet, which seems odd. Wouldn't a father immediately realize his daughter is nearby?

"Why would he?"

I can't answer that. It simply strikes me as odd.

"Be on your guard then. The smallest thing moves and we will attack. We have fought ship-board before."

I draw in a breath as Stekkan moves, pushing through

the ring of guarding bodies. One of them cries out but Stekkan's Nakuraki strikes, silencing the sailor with a quick blow to the throat. He falls to his knees, hands clasped around his neck choking.

"Eyes up. He is not your concern."

Guilt floods over me. We don't know that the sailors are turned. That could be an innocent man who was struck just now but .... wait ... wait. There is something odd about him. Something shimmery. Something that, now that I notice it, is true of all the sailors ringing this tableau. True — even — of my father. I reach up to rub my eyes. Perhaps it is merely exhaustion catching up with me. Perhaps.

"I ... cannot advise. I have not seen this ... I do not remember this."

Vargaard sounds lost, and for just a second I feel a spike of fear. We've walked right in here counting on his sage advice and his experience. But what if he's already lost too much of both?

"I will not let you go."

But will that be enough? I want to claw that back as soon as it slips out, but it is too late. One glance at my Vargaard shows me his clamped jaw and stoic expression.

I'm sorry, I'm so sorry.

"It's nothing."

But we both know that is a lie. It was not nothing and he is not acting as though it is. I have hurt him with a stray thought.

"You're right. It is not nothing. It is deadly accurate. I own to it entirely."

I will have to patch this later. There is no time right now.

Head held high, Vargaard finds his place hovering at my side where he can watch my back and front both at once. My shadow is mostly behind me. He will have little room to maneuver if a threat comes from the front. I find my place at Stekkan's shoulder, trying to be as visible as possible as he continues his saunter into the warmth of the ring of lantern light in the center of the boat.

Stekkan crosses into the light, his shadow streaming behind him like the banner of a conqueror, head held high, chest thrust outward. Were an artist to carve a scene for *Conquering King and His Supplicants* for the woodcut of a history book, this is the exact attitude they would put him in. All he lacks is a crown, and in this light, it is easy to imagine.

For a moment, all is silent and every breath held except the slapping of the waves against the hull of the boat and the distant sound of mirth from the other ships in the flotilla. Here, on this ship, you can hear every squeak of board on board, every sound of a rope tightening. The breeze kicks up across the river, snapping the flags and canvas and catching the hair of the surrounding guards and sailors, blowing it in faces and teeth.

I look from my frozen father to my frozen queen, to the ring of frozen sailors around us. They look shocked to see us as if no one could expect anyone to arrive on an unguarded deck.

Am I seeing things? Is this not real? It looks like a dream. Feels like one, too. The only real thing is Stekkan before me, jaw pronounced as he grits his teeth and lifts his ceremonial sword.

"It's real," Vargaard assures me. *"But it's wrong. Somehow, it is wrong."*

The ship sways and something rolls across the table from Jendaya's opened fingers making a wobbling sound. Its course is determined by the knots in the wood and the edges of the map, and yet — exactly as I knew he would — my father's meaty hand darts out faster than a seagull and snatches it up and I see only a glint of green from between his thick fingers. My breath catches in my throat. The green gem.

"Wife," Stekkan says to Jendaya, his voice sounding too loud in the silence. "It seems you've started this party without me."

His words break the silence and around us the ring of — guards? sailors? witnesses? — breaks out into nervous laughter.

"Well, I did look," Jendaya drawls, exaggerating her lounge as she settles even further back into a stout ship's chair. "I looked and looked, but when you marry a rabbit, you must expect to give him a merry chase, is that not right, Prince of Cragspear?"

"I heard rumors it was 'King' now."

Neither of them is watching my father. I can't take my eyes off him. His gaze darts from Stekkan to Jendaya and back but he does not look at me. I can smell the taramoc and tobacco on him and still he does not look at me. I shrug his old coat over my shoulders. Finally, his eyes sweep over me.

Oh. The Tranquility Sword. I have been gripping the hilt without realizing it. I release the hilt and the moment I become visible my father's eyes widen and his chair scrapes back as he rises to his feet.

"Ilsaletta," he says, his eyes lighting up. And I feel myself melt as his smile widens, feel all my troubles lessening. He spreads his arms wide. "My darling girl! You are alive!"

My chest swells and my eyes prick slightly and my grin is wide as I stumble toward him and then — out of nowhere — I am pushed violently backward into the chest of one of the sailors. I catch his confused cry as he stumbles backward, leaving me to find my own feet, catch the glimpse of fear on Vargaard's shadow face for only a moment — and then my shadow guardian is spinning around again.

But why has he thrown me backward? Is he ... could he be jealous of my loyalties?

A growl rumbles in his mind and he curls his lip and points his blade at the same moment that my father's confused expression melts to understanding and he shrugs helplessly.

Vargaard's blade is pointed to where a small, brown sugar colored glow slips out my father's sleeve and runs up my father's arm. A smoke mouse. A tiny one.

And this horrible revelation is so opposite to my lion of a father that I can't help myself.

I laugh.

CHAPTER SIXTEEN

"Oh, so we'll be playing happy families then," Jendaya says, lifting her goblet of wine and draining it completely. "How lovely. The last time I did this it led to a very pointed succession, but perhaps things will be different now that we're playing with a second family. What do you say, Admiral Redtide. You aren't planning to slump off and leave this world, are you? I guess you'll just have to wait for your turn, Ilsa, love."

She laughs as if she's said something funny and refills her goblet, but I find no mirth in the past murder of her father, nor in the joking implication that she might do the same to mine.,

"You did not tell me that my daughter lived, Queen Jendaya," my father says and for the first time in my life, I cannot read his face. I cannot tell what turbulent emotion that is behind his eyes. There is a flicker of something that looks as if it might be anger or possibly doubt. And a flicker of something else — like rolling breakers in the sea

— a sadness similar to that his face takes on when he speaks of my mother.

"You did not ask," she says.

"With *my* wife," Stekkan says, stepping forward and snatching his wife's cup from the table.

She leaps from her chair at his approach like a mouse darting away from a cat, fully vaulting backward over the chair back and retreating two paces before Stekkan's hand even wraps around the stem of her goblet.

He freezes, bemused, as her unicorn shoots out between them, and her guards crowd around her, drawing their swords and forming up in a three-layer formation where the front layer kneels, the second squats, and the third stands firm, but all hold their blades balanced facing outward at chest level.

Undaunted, Stekkan swallows the wine, clears his throat, and then finishes his sentence. "As I was saying, with my wife you should always ask. Or don't. Her reactions if you don't can be amusing. That was a very quick retreat for someone who told me only days ago that arms like mine are fit for nothing but holding women."

"That was flattery," Jendaya spits. She's trembling and I don't know if it's with rage or fear or passion.

"That was optimism," Stekkan's half-smirk is disdainful.

"I feel I have intruded on a domestic dispute," my father says warily. "It was my understanding that you came here to accept my fealty, Queen Jendaya."

"You don't have to give it to her," I say, heart wrenching within me. I barely notice as Vargaard sweeps behind me, tackling a sailor who was reaching for my throat. I hear the sailor's pitiful scream followed by a splash. He has gotten off lightly, even if he hits a boat on the way down.

My father sucks in his lower lip before his eyes narrow and he speaks, but he does not open his arms to me again. Instead, he cocks his head to one side and the look in his eyes tells me he is doing very quick calculations.

"What would you have me do, daughter? The dice are tossed and have come down upon the table. The bets have been placed. There is nothing now but to play the game."

I shake my head as another scream erupts from behind me. I hope Vargaard is having fun, at least.

"It is not fun to watch your heart shatter."

It is not fun to *have* my heart shatter.

"I would have you be the father I thought you were," I plead with my father, grabbing the lapels of his coat that I am still wearing — road stains and all —- and shaking them as if to show them to him. "The one I thought was coming to save me. The one I expected to be unassailable by evil. I have tried to keep faith with you. Will you not keep faith with me?"

His voice is almost tender in its sorrow as he says, "And who is this paragon of men with whom you keep faith?"

"You!" My voice is thick with emotion.

And so is his. He must clear his throat to get the words out.

"It is not me, girl dear."

Jendaya laughs from her sword cocoon. "You're the most ungrateful girl, Ilsaletta. I would have killed for a father like yours. I did, actually. Mine was a sniveling fool. Yours, on the other hand, will help to lead Cragspear into a new age. While the other nations are still flinching from their bouts of plague, we will stride forward on land and sea with purpose and commitment."

She clenches one fist as if she's giving a speech to rally her troops. Perhaps she is. She's as dramatic as Stekkan.

"Not if I scuttle your ships first," I threaten, leaning forward and hunching over my sword in my rage. I hear another scream from behind me and a curse from Vargaard.

"Seriously, Ilsaletta — it won't work if you warn them!"

"Our ships are unscuttleable." Jendaya pauses. "Is that a word?"

"It is in the way that you're a queen," Stekkan says easily with a sigh afterward as if he's bored.

He drags the chair she'd been sitting in across the boat deck very noisily and sits on it, throwing his feet up on the table, laying his naked sword over his legs, and sloshing wine from a pitcher into her goblet. Behind him, his Naku-raki is working as hard as Vargaard to keep back the sailors and guards making attempts on his life. I wish I were not so tormented so that I could enjoy this new King Stekkan.

"I rather like him this way, myself."

"Be calm, Ilsaletta," my father tries to say, as if I am a child he is dealing with and not a woman who has realized who he is. "You are newly infected. The sickness will pass through you, and then you will understand. I know that, like me, you will survive and you will master it."

Jendaya laughs. "I swear, I haven't laughed this hard in

ages. Perhaps I should tell you, Admiral Redtide, that your daughter was among those *first* infected."

"I don't understand." A furrow is forming in his forehead.

"Then you didn't go back to Saltfast?" I ask carefully.

He shakes his head. "I had orders to repair to Swordheart immediately on arrival. We received messenger birds at the port."

"Amongst the dead," I say hollowly.

"The dead are the weak ones, my girl. You will not be so weak." His voice is a growl.

Jendaya snickers, "I think you should tell him, Ilsaletta. I like watching hearts broken almost as much as I like breaking them."

"You don't have to do this," Vargaard tells me. *"Let's surprise them and jump ship."*

But I'm not ready to do that yet. Not when my father is still clutching that green gem. If we could get out hands on that, it would change everything.

"The dead *are* the weak," I agree, feeling the blood rush to my cheeks. "And we perish for it. But only because their moral lack has cracked the world wide open like an egg. Tell me, my father, what do you think it means that you are not dead? Who are these ones who bubble with pillars of smoke, their faces split in two?"

"They're the ones who survived," my father says, tapping his thigh with a finger.

Behind me, there is another strangled scream. Is he giving signals to his men to capture me? He is only ordering their deaths.

"Order your men off, Admiral. It's annoying to watch them killed by spirits," Jendaya's voice is grim but she turns a tight smile to Stekkan. "And who would have thought you'd acquire a Nakuraki, husband? Almost, you are worthy of me."

I nearly miss Stekkan's retort as it is masked by another scream. "But you'll never be worthy of me, Jendaya, Queen of corpses. Isn't that right, Mercy?"

"Mercy! Mercy!" his bird screams, sailing a ring over us before settling on Stekkan's shoulder and preening. He reaches up an idle hand to caress where feathers ought to be.

My father makes a snapping motion with his fingers, calling his sailors off, I think. Confusion is writ large on his face, but when I turn to look over my shoulder, I see three of his sailors are blooming, their faces beginning to crack, smoke pouring through the fissures. I spin back to my father and see his face growing pale, his knuckles white on the green gem.

"Some of my sailors are not disciplined," my father admits with a twist of his mouth his eyes meeting mine guiltily. "Life on the seas draws many types. But we've seen that those with a will can master this madness. Look at your queen and her avatar. Look at me, with mine. You will be the same, daughter."

The smoke mouse scurries a circle around his neck twice and I shiver.

Ilsaletta, Vargaard says carefully in my mind. *Your father is not a good man.*

I laugh a little hysterically. Obviously. Were he a good

man, he would not have a smoke mouse running around his neck.

"Surely, it is a sign of your discipline that you remain intact if you were exposed days ago," my father says reasonably. "Show me your smoke avatar. It is no shame if it is small. My own is but a mouse. It has not hindered my ability to fight with it."

I feel ill. I am going to vomit.

Stekkan turns to meet my eye and the pity within his nearly makes me crumple. He knows exactly how I feel, for he is in love with an evil woman, just like I adore an evil man — a man who raised me and taught me everything.

Stekkan lifts an eyebrow. Our plan is out the window. My father is no ally to us. Clearly, he wants to know if I will back whatever play he has devised next, pushed on by the bizarre confidence of his sword. I steel my jaw. My answer will be in my words to my father and after this, we two will be enemies. I dare not leave anything unsaid. I draw in a long breath.

"Look at the King of Cragspear," I tell my father gently. My mouth twists bitterly, tears beginning to form — but they are not the tears of sorrow alone. They are laden with fury.

"That popinjay who was once the Duke of Catterail?" My father laughs as if this is a joke. It is no joke. And I do not find him humorous. "My Queen may marry as she pleases and as many as she pleases. I do not need to give her poppets any mind."

I clench my jaw and spit my words with vigor.

"Popinjay or not, Stekkan Duke of Catterrail, King of

Cragspear is a good man." And now my tears spring up and flow down my cheeks and my whole body shaking with my furious indignation. My father has betrayed my heart. "He is a good man." I point at Stekkan with the tip of my sword. "Him. And you are not. How can this be?"

"A good man?" My father raises an eyebrow at me and Jendaya's laugh is low as if she is enjoying every moment of this. "I won't tolerate more of this outburst Ilsaletta. Sheathe that blade and come sit with us."

"I *did* marry a good man," Jendaya muses. "I find it endlessly amusing. The things he *won't* do are almost as interesting as what he will. Besides, it turns out he's a rarity."

My father looks at her, puzzled, and then at me.

"Is it possible," I ask carefully, "that no one amongst all your sailors remained alive but unturned by the plague?"

My father's jaw tightens. I have displeased him.

"We lost many good men." Clearly his definition of 'good' is different than mine. "But of those left, all have mastered the plague or been mastered by it. No one remains the same, Ilsaletta. It is not possible."

"I am the same." My lips are thick as I say this, twisting with bitterness.

His eyes meet mine — open and vulnerable for a moment before they shutter off all emotion.

"Not possible, my girl."

"It is possible," I say quietly. If pain has a flavor it is stomach acid. "Those who are good survived this intact. They are fewer than I imagined."

"One in ten," Stekkan adds helpfully, pouring more wine.

My eyes, however, are trained on my father when I say, "Far fewer than I'd hoped."

"What are you saying?" The familiar love has left my father's eyes. They are hardening.

"What do you think I'm saying?" My voice breaks at the end and my father's answering grunt guts me.

A sickly sense of anticipation fills me. So, this is what it feels like to be the enemy of Admiral Redtide.

Vargaard slips around me, flickering in front of me as he senses this change in the dynamics. He's been very quiet.

"Unlike Jendaya, I do not enjoy watching hearts broken. Certainly not yours, my sun, my stars."

His shadow hand flicks out as if he would like to take mine, but it closes on nothing, just as always, and my heart is hollow, hollow, hollow.

Stekkan clears his throat. "Well, this has been nice, but I suppose we'd better be off."

Jendaya barks a laugh. "I think not."

And her words are echoed by my father. "Those are not terms I accept."

And then, to my utter shock, Stekkan's Nakuraki rushes toward Jendaya's throat and he leaps from his chair to follow her.

CHAPTER SEVENTEEN

"Back! Back! To the left!" Vargaard coaches me.

Complete chaos has unfolded like a napkin before a feast. Stekkan's Nakuraki is tearing into Jendaya's guards like a dog through a nest of ducks and he's hard on her heels. Mercy screams from just over his head, flying loops over the charge like an enraged hornet.

Stekkan is fighting.

Stekkan is charging into danger. It boggles the mind.

I quickly follow Vargaard's instructions, until I realize he isn't taking me deeper into the battle, he's trying to maneuver me off the ship, and I'm not ready to go yet.

Not without that gem.

I pause and then I step smartly toward my father as my Nakuraki curses loudly in my head.

"One last embrace? Daughter to father?" I ask, speaking loudly to draw my father's gaze away from the chaos of Jendaya and Stekkan.

"It is unwise to take your eyes off of a fight so close nearby! You could be killed by accident."

I hope he guards my back well, then.

"Ilsaletta! Please, it cannot be worth it!" Vargaard is pleading.

I say to my father, "Will you not bid me farewell?"

Admiral Redtide finally rips his eyes away from the conflict and they flick to me, but he is still as if trying to think of too many things at once. His fingers flick in a way that might be signals to someone or simply a nervous tick. I see it in his face the moment he realizes this cannot possibly be about daughterly love.

I reach for his palm in a last desperate bid, and his eyes widen as he jerks his hand back.

"Ilsaletta!" he admonishes me. "Is this what you want? The Queen's treasure? I did not think you to be so grasping. And here I promised your betrothed that you were a well-mannered, quiet slip of a girl."

"Betrothed," Vargaard spits. *"Let me guess, he's around here somewhere with a smoke rat."*

"I was once well-mannered and quiet," I agree, dancing forward, unwilling to let go of his wrist with my free hand. If I have that gem, then I can ... well, I don't know, but if it caused all this then it must also fix it."

"Anything arising from that artifact can only be evil."

Vargaard seems distracted and then he grunts and that is enough to call my attention back. I release my father and twist so I can see him. He's surrounded by sailors, all of them having fledged into true husks now, their freshly rent faces horrific as smoke puffs up from them in unfettered clouds.

Without thinking, I dart forward, sword at the ready.

"Not my men!" my father shouts as my blade bites deep.

Vargaard has thrust a man upon my blade and is reaching for another. I wrench my sword from the first man's belly only to feel something wrap around my waist and yank me back suddenly. Vargaard loses his grip, sliding with my shadow across the ship deck.

The arms around my belly are my father's. He is my enemy now.

"Enough of this," Jendaya yells and I spare her a glance. Most of her physical guard is down, writhing on the deck, but her sword is drawn and Haszinth, sixth of his name, is pounding Stekkan's Nakuraki with blow after blow. "Toss me the gem, Admiral."

"When his grip loosens, raise your arms and drop!" Vargaard's words are quick and sharp and the second my father's grip loosens, I hurry to obey, dropping from his arms to the deck.

"Roll! Roll!"

I roll until my back hits the rail and then I scramble to my feet, but not before the riverboat lurches, sending me reeling, gripping the railing with both hands.

Over the railing? Do we jump?

"Not now. Sweet Fisher King, not now."

I look up to see Vargaard beside me, holding a hand out as if he could steady me, his mouth wide with surprise. I follow his gaze and gasp along with him.

Jendaya has wrenched the Tenacity Sword from Stekkan's hand and jammed it into the green gem and just like that, the Nakuraki bursts into flames, and with a scream, she disappears and her sword turns suddenly into perfect sword-formed dust and then falls in a pathetic rain to the deck.

I'm shaking all over as I meet Vargaard's eyes.

"Jump."

I thought he said not to jump.

My eyes are on Stekkan, lying on his back on the deck, trembling as he drags himself backward in an awkward crab crawl. Jendaya draws her Spirit Sword.

"I wasn't talking to you when I said that. Jump! Jump while you can!"

And then Jendaya spins the Spirit Sword in a massive arc and a sound like a rock dropped from a wall and striking the earth fills our ears and then the air in front of the boat rips in two like a sheet ripped for rags and the edges flutter, flame-edged and ragged.

"Throw off!" my father's order booms out, and to my horror, the lines connecting us to the other boat are thrown over the side.

"Jump!" Vargaard says as a screaming spirit macaw lands on my shoulder, shrieking furiously.

I want to stay and grab Stekkan, but I have learned my lesson about ignoring Vargaard. I climb up the rail as fast as I can as the boat lurches forward.

I swing one leg over the rail, determination gripping me where all my senses are fleeing in fear. I do not enjoy heights. I swing the other over, sheathe the Mercy Sword and I'm just about to leap when Vargaard whispers.

"*Too late! Do not leap, my Ilsaletta!*"

The sound of crunching bones fills the air and a bright light floods my vision and then — as sudden as falling into a dream — we are no longer on the river.

The ship is still sailing. Still moving. Like ice forming over the top of a bucket in winter, something white builds up, crusting over the entire boat and when I look down at where my feet are perched I nearly jerk them upward when I see what it is. Ivory-white bones interwoven with the writhing dead have grown over the hull like a layer of barnacles. Every inch of the boat is encrusted with them.

I'm still gaping when I look up and the light fades enough to see around us.

Jendaya has sailed us straight into the Sea of Souls and we ride on the waves of those who were once human.

CHAPTER EIGHTEEN

"I told you my ship was unscuttleable," Jendaya says smugly, but her eyes are wild and too bright — even here where the light somehow washes all color out, leaving everything grim shades of black, white, and grey.

Screams meet my ears — so many that they sound almost like a terrible wind in a storm, howling, roaring, moaning.

"Bring your feet to the other side of the railing before you're pulled ... before you fall off," Vargaard says.

I start to move, but something tugs me suddenly from below and my foot is pulled downward. I grip the railing with both hands as I'm drawn down hard. My fingers slip on the slick railing. I'm losing my grip. I'm going to fall. My heart is in my throat.

I look down to see what is below me and wish I had not. It is the Sea of Souls as seen from above. People stacked on people, stacked on people, writhing, screaming, moaning, clawing — a swell of souls, furious, angry, desperate, despairing. My mind is swollen with the sensation of it.

They're going to swallow me alive.

It is from this mass of souls that the tumultuous noise boils upward.

The ship plows through their depths, riding on and over backs and heads and limbs and if it leaves a crushed wake behind it, I cannot tell because any space it clears is immediately swollen full of more souls.

I scream at the sight, my voice tearing from my lungs as if plucked away by a vengeful spirit.

Mercy screams, too, and I feel her kick off my shoulder, her feathers brushing my face as she takes off with screams of, *"Mercy! Mercy! Mercy for the dead!"*

And then Vargaard is beside me, leaning over the rail, his sword fast as lightning as it strikes the man gripping my foot and rends his arm clean from his body. The pressure lessens and I scramble to find purchase as I clutch the boat rail, and then suddenly I'm being drawn up by strong arms — up and over the rail. I gasp when my foot clears. I fall forward so quickly that we both topple in a heap and I'm face to face with Vargaard. He's beneath me, all muscles and hard planes.

I can feel his breath on my face.

I can feel his heart beating.

I can feel his warmth.

I reach for him, tenderly, softly, and I just manage to run my fingers over his chiseled cheek and press my lips softly to his when he fades back to a spirit and I fall heavily to the deck.

"Oh, Ilsaletta! I'm sorry, I'm so sorry," he gasps.

I hope he's sorry that he faded away and not that I kissed him.

"Look at me."

I look at him and see him there, crouched beside me. There are no shadows here, but I do not think he needs one in this realm for it is the realm of the dead, and that makes it his. He has two fingers pressed to his lips as if he can hold my kiss there, keep it as a token.

I do not want to think about the horrors that surround us. I want only to think of this. I want to hold it between us. Forever.

"So do I."

Pain hits me in the side — sharp and sudden. It rips up my arm and across my neck and I'm starting to scream when Vargaard explodes to his feet and his sword slashes out toward my face. I let the scream fly from my lips at the same moment that something pale and fuzzy falls to the ground.

My father's spirit mouse has been stabbed by my guardian Nakuraki.

Vargaard skewers it on the end of his blade and lifts it up at the same moment that he reaches to help me stand, and his hand goes right through me. His smile is wry. Whatever changed for us here for just a few moments is gone now. And whatever was different when he carried me through this world — one spirit clasping another — is also different when I am here in body. The old rules still apply.

I stand by my own power and find my father facing me grimly.

"Queen Jendaya has given me the Dead Seas," he calls over the noisy tumult.

"It's the Sea of Souls," I reply calmly, but he either doesn't care or doesn't hear.

"As Admiral of the Dead Seas, it is my duty to disarm all aboard and compel you to serve or step overboard." His booming voice has no problem slicing through the background noise.

"If there was doubt before about your father's heart, I see no reason to doubt now," Vargaard says and I cannot help but agree.

My father is a practical man. It seems he has chosen the most practical course for himself. If you must be dead and fouled, then why not be on top, too?

"Even your daughter?" I have to raise my voice to push back. But I will push back. Perhaps he can still see sense. "You attacked me with that mouse!"

"Is that not *my* sword from *my* locked box in your scabbard?" My father asks me and I know the hard look in his eye. It brooks no defiance. It allows no discussion. He cannot be persuaded.

"You already tried persuasion. I suggest a different tack," Vargaard says.

But my father's words have reminded me of something. I do not have only one sword in my belt, do I?

I switch grips on my sword, moving it to the other hand, and I see my father's eyes narrow in confusion at the same time that Jendaya screams — "Watch her!"

I draw the Tenacity Sword in one smooth motion and as the White Lady arrives, I leap to the side.

The world feels slow and thick, as though I wade through batts of wool. I sheathe the Mercy Sword with what feels like it should be speed but is, instead, impossibly slow. Beside me, my father lumbers forward to where I should be and then suddenly his hands have the book strapped to my back in his grip, and he's blindly wrenching at it with all his might. The strap snaps and the book comes loose.

Vargaard's foot slides out and kicks my father's knee — hard — and he goes down in a heap.

I feel my breath catch.

"Spare no pity for he who would not pity you."

I'm hesitating, eyes on the book.

"Leave it for now. You don't have enough hands."

I'll have to recover it after — whatever this is. I don't dare lose it. My heart is in my throat as I spare a last glance for my father. He has the book clutched to his chest.

He is not dead. I should not judge my guardian for protecting me. And yet there is something that feels wrong about turning on my father. The way it would feel wrong for my own hand to turn on me.

"He is the one who turned, Ilsaletta. You are not the betrayer here."

He's right. He's always right. His advice is laced with generations of wisdom.

"Not anymore. I grasp and they run through my fingers as water."

Well, he's still wiser than I am.

"I will not argue with that."

As we've been talking, I've been picking my way as

silently as possible around the edge of the flat riverboat deck. It's designed to carry cargo but is currently empty except for the tables and chairs from Jendaya and my father's meeting. The only one hatch leading below is shut. There's a tiller at the back and a raised platform for the tiller man. It's currently unmanned. Either the boat is drifting as it wills on the Sea of Souls or is directed by some other means.

There are — perhaps — half a dozen guards left on board. The lonely remaining sailor moves to help my father and yelps when a smoke salamander darts from his hand and dissipates. Well. That seals it. Admiral Redtide, man of honor and repute, scourge of the seas, pride of Cragspear, managed to do what seems almost impossible. He did not have a single good man in his employ.

My eyes sweep the deck.

"Watch your feet."

I carefully maneuver around a coiled rope and a cask, keeping my footsteps as quiet as possible. Already, my father's eyes are sweeping the deck with a coldly calculating gleam in them. That he would look at *me* that way chills me.

"If you feel there is an imbalance of death glares, I can even that out."

I smile slightly at that. The world is thick with the fog of the Tranquility Sword, everything seeming to happen in the slowest manner possible. I know it is an illusion when I see Jendaya's guards spread out around her like a fanning flower — but a flower of treacle petals where each one slowly slumps into place. Were I not holding the sword and absorbing its calm, they would fan out the same as normal.

Jendaya's flick of the wrist displays the green gem in one hand. The movement is as slow as moving through butter. Her other hand holds a knife that tickles the edge of Stekkan's jaw so sluggishly that it looks more like flirting than a threat. But even swathed in tranquility, I know better. The fear in his eyes is real. The strength in her actions, just as real.

If I could just get close, in past her guard, perhaps I could end this now. I could take the gem. I could take her life. It could all be over.

"And the Nakuraki remaining, the corricles and husks, will continue to ravage your world. I do not think the death of one golden-haired queen will stop this."

He's right. I steel my jaw. Then for now, my best bet is escape with Stekkan, until such a time as we can regroup and plot a new course.

"Yes."

I edge so close to the rail that I see them when they emerge. Farrakki — the dread creatures of Jendaya — are rising up in the tide of human souls and surrounding the boat, buoying it higher as their strange, unreal bodies push against the sides.

"They are a good reminder that Jendaya always has more allies nearby than you expect. Even here, in the Sea of Souls."

I cannot leap over the side. And I do not know how to get back to the land of the living.

"Perhaps by the same means we arrived here? Perhaps you can slash a hole in the world and simply step through."

With the Tranquility Sword?

"No. You'll need Jendaya's Spirit Sword."

The one with Haszinth in it. The Nakuraki who hates it.

"He must serve the wielder."

I bite the inside of my lip as I think of that. It has more implications than can be grasped in the heat of the moment.

My father is barking something at Jendaya but to my ears, his words come so slowly that I cannot comprehend them. She leans forward and says something back and at her words, Stekkan drops to his knees, but the drop seems to take an hour as I slide through air thick as eiderdown.

"She cannot hold three things at once. She will not drop the gem. If she..."

Before Vargaard's thought is finished, Jendaya's knife begins to fall, heedless of where it might land and she reaches for her Spirit Sword.

"Go! Now!" Vargaard urges me and I leap forward as fast as I can under the effects of tranquility. The moment Jendaya's hand reaches that hilt, she will be able to see us even if no one else does.

Too much is happening at once.

The moment my shadow crosses one of Jendaya's guards, Vargaard reaches out and snaps his neck. It seems to happen with painful slowness.

Jendaya's knife is still tumbling down to where Stekkan crouches on the deck.

Her hand is a breath away from her hilt.

I claw through the air, not fast enough, not fast enough. I am beyond concern for the sound of my feet slapping the deck. I will have one chance at this.

But even as Vargaard kills a second guard, even as I hear Stekkan scream begin as the tip of Jendaya's blade bites the back of his hand and begins to penetrate his flesh, Jendaya's fingers find the hilt of her sword.

Haszinth shoots out from her shadow like an arrow loosed.

My heart is in my throat as he lunges toward me, fast despite the slowness of everything. I get both blades out in front of me but they're slow, so, so slow.

Vargaard is moving to try to get between us.

Haszinth's grin widens.

He strikes out — fast, even here in a land of quicksand and packing wool. His Spirit Sword comes down so hard on my Tranquility Sword that it falls from my hand. Pain shoots up my wrist. My father gasps from behind me somewhere.

The sword tumbles and strikes the ship deck with a clatter, landing right beside Stekkan who is pinned to the deck — a knife in his hand. Vargaard slides between Haszinth and me with a flexing twist, easily turning Haszinth's follow up blow, his sword whipping out and spinning around Haszinth's Spirit Sword before twisting in a way that pulls the other Nakuraki, elongating his shadow.

I will Stekkan to snatch up the Tranquility Sword as I lurch forward. He's reaching for it with his offhand, his dominant — and closest hand — still pinned by the knife.

But just as his fingers brush it, another hand scoops it up. Haszinth vanishes in a sudden puff, and Jendaya, with a look of triumph on her face, plunges the Tranquility Sword into the green gem. The white lady's last scream is silent as she tears into shreds and is gone. The sword vanishes in ash and dust.

"Haven't you realized by now that I don't need these trinkets or their lurid guardians?" Jendaya asks as she turns to me. "Haven't you realized that you can't bring them all together if I destroy even one of them?"

But I have not been idle. The moment Haszinth vanished, I leapt forward and now my leap is nearly complete. Nearly, but not quite. Jendaya fumbles for the Spirit Sword and my heart is in my throat. She's going to get it and stop me before I reach her.

Like a thunderbolt from the sky a white shape swoops in screaming, "Mercy! Mercy!" as it attacks Jendaya's face in a flurry of claws and feathers and it's all the distraction that I need. I barrel into Jendaya, knock her backward into one of her frozen guards, his mouth a wild "O" of shock, and as we fall together, I reach for the hilt by her side.

"Hold onto the hilt and twist your whole body to the right as hard as you can!"

Vargaard's order splits through all else and I hurry to obey, twisting and pulling with all my might.

The sword springs free with a *zing* and as it frees from the scabbard, it slices an arc through the air and my breath rips from my chest as it opens the black and white of the Seas of Souls up into the terrible verdant brightness of the living world.

A sword blade crashes down beside my head, wedging in the wood of the boat deck with a *thunk.* A glint off the blade nearly blinds me, it's so close to my face. I see my own eye in the smooth metal.

I gasp and then a hand wrenches me up and I know I must not drop the swords. I must not. I grip them tightly and my feet flounder to find purchase as I'm ripped upward to my feet.

I expect to see Vargaard hauling me up, or possibly even my father.

I do not expect a wild-eyed Stekkan, the dagger still pierced right through his palm. He tosses me through the rent in the air and it's all I can do not to skewer myself with the swords I clutch in each fist as I try to keep my feet. And then I'm caught in shadow arms, and we twist through the air violently as Vargaard whispers.

"Let your body go slack. I'll catch the blades and the blow."

We tumble through the air, I go slack, and the world goes dark.

CHAPTER NINETEEN

I blink twice and Stekkan has ripped the Spirit Sword from my hand and is closing the slash in the air. He breathes hard, breath coming out in rough puffs. We're somewhere dark and there are white splashes of stars overhead. Something sways nearby. The world smells of the sea.

And I'm paying attention to none of it, because wrapped around me are Vargaard's arms and under me is his heaving chest and I can feel it *all*. He's warm, and alive, and solid and I push away everything, all the raw pain, and fear, and ... everything ... and refuse to give it any purchase because I want just one selfish moment of everything. I let go of the Mercy Sword, turn in his arms and feel them flex tightly around me. He's squeezing the breath out of me with his desperate full-body embrace, curling around me even though he's the one lying against the ground.

I find his face in the darkness and I'm slain by the rough gasp that tears through his parted lips. In the faint light of the stars, I find his lips with my own and sink into them, sliding my lips across them, gentle with my devoted kisses. He kisses me back, making sounds in the back of his throat that are hungry and wanting and my head is whirling, my fingers sliding up his cheeks and tangling into his hair. I've never felt anything like this. I think my heart will explode. I might be crying and I don't care. I just want more of him. All of him.

And then suddenly he's gone and I fall against the earth with smashing force and my lip strikes something hard. I taste blood.

My fingers fly up to my bleeding lip.

"Serves you right," Stekkan says as I push myself up. I can just barely make him out in the starlight. He's squatting nearby. "I should know. Every time I give in to passion it only ever makes me bleed, too."

"That doesn't sound at all bitter," I remark, my voice muffled by my attempt to wipe the earth out of my mouth. I think it was a tree root that bruised my lips.

"You have my apologies, Ilsaletta. It was poorly done of me. I should have realized what might happen when I faded again."

If he apologizes for the greatest moment of my life again I will be very irritated.

He gives a wary mental laugh.

"The greatest moment?"

By far.

"Then tell Stekkan that if he mocks you again, he'll find it isn't just passion that makes him bleed."

"Where are we?" I ask Stekkan instead.

He snorts. "How would I know?"

On his shoulder, his spirit bird glows brightly, pacing back and forth across his shoulders and a dagger still sticks out of his hand.

I want to snap back at him. The events on the ship have left me raw and miserable, and the sudden taste of Vargaard snatched away too soon has left little shivers of frustration under my skin.

Instead, I say, "Let's take a look at your hand."

He offers me the Spirit Sword and I take it without thinking, meaning to sheathe it, only to freeze at the stream of horrific curses flung at me by the Nakuraki trapped in the sword. He lunges toward me, screaming obscenities, his spirit face warped and distorted. It is only Vargaard's quick thinking that pushes him back. My Nakuraki's hand wraps around the other shadow's throat and shoves him back a step and then back another.

I sheathe the blade into the Tranquility Sword's sheath. It's an ill fit but it will have to do.

I sag with relief as his shadow vanishes.

"Well," I say a little queasily. "I think I could do without him." Vargaard breathes out a long breath and I fumble in my pouch for tinder and a stub of candle. "I'll light a candle so we can see your hand."

"He shouldn't be able to do that. He should be bound to you."

If Vargaard thinks that worries him, I'm doubly worried. I don't dare do so much as brush the hilt of that sword or risk Haszinth throttling me. I clench my jaw hard. The last few hours have been … too much.

"Your father's betrayal has wounded you deeply. You

could not have realized ahead of time, and now that you know his heart, you cannot bring him back."

Logically, that should absolve me of guilt. But it does not. I should have realized who my father was, shouldn't I? I am his daughter. I was raised by him. How could I have been so blind?

I try to calm myself by focusing on Stekkan's condition instead. When lit, the candle gives off a circle of bobbing light, illuminating the queasy expression on Stekkan's face. I think it might be an exact match for mine.

"Here," I say gently. "Hold the Mercy Sword. It will dull the pain."

He takes it eagerly. His lovely face is drawn and miserable.

"I was a fool to plunge us into that," he admits.

"I'm not sure that's true."

But he is inconsolable. "Look what we lost! The Tranquility Sword. The Tenacity Sword — that's two weapons we could have used! You had meant to collect all seven, I know it. You had hoped to unite them to defeat Jendaya, but she's taken that chance from us. And we've lost the tome, too." He shaking now — either with emotion or in shock from what has just occurred.

"Try to stay calm," I say as I examine his hand. The wound looks clean enough, and the knife has somehow — miraculously — missed bone, but this is not my specialty.

"No, it's his," Vargaard reminds me. *"He is the one with medical training. Perhaps he has advice for you."*

Vargaard is hovering behind me, likely guarding us from the shadows. I glance over my shoulder at him and gasp. He's illuminated by the candlelight and there are wounds marring his lovely face. He is shadow still, but he does not flicker from form to form and a wound is in the shadow of his forehead, bleeding shadow blood down his face. There is a tear in the jacket across his chest.

"You're wounded," I gasp.

"Yes, shocking, I know," Stekkan says wryly. "Who would have thought that a knife in the hand would hurt."

"I was speaking to my shadow guardian. You are not the only human alive, Stekkan, King of Cragspear," I say wryly and Stekkan has the grace to look away with embarrassment.

"*Do not trouble yourself over me.*"

Vargaard does not seem concerned about his wounds, but even if he were, there's little I can do for him. If I cannot touch him, then I cannot help him. I bite my lip and turn back to Stekkan.

"*I admit to being torn, my book girl. If I am flesh, then I can be wounded and killed, and therefore, I am less help to you, less of a guardian, less of a wall against trouble. But if I am flesh ... then I can love you tenderly. I know not which I need most.*"

I do not look back at him when I say in my mind, "*I know which I need.*"

"Just ease the knife out in the exact direction it entered," Stekkan tells me, gripping the Mercy Sword hard to ease his pain. "Then you'll stitch the skin with the needle and thread in my belt pouch and we'll wrap it in my handkerchief."

"I wish we could do better for you," I murmur as I

reach to draw the needle and thread from his belt pouch. I must lean in very close to do it and I feel as though I am intruding on his person.

"I don't think we have that kind of friendship," he says and his expression is dry. I think he's joking but I don't know what he means.

"He's suggesting that you might ... kiss his worries away," Vargaard tells me. He sounds uncomfortable.

After he just witnessed me try to kiss Vargaard and get my lip bloodied for my efforts?

"Try? That was very much a success."

I had thought that now he was married, Stekkan would stop teasing me.

"I'm not entirely certain he can ever stop teasing people. He's not a man made for faithfulness," Vargaard says.

I disagree. He is entirely faithful to Mercy.

"A bird."

Yes, but if you couldn't be faithful to the most weak and vulnerable, the least powerful on their own, then were you really faithful at all?

"I stand corrected."

He pauses as I draw the knife slowly from Stekkan's hand. Stekkan hisses through his teeth, his cheek flinching in a pained tick.

Vargaard's words, when they come, are laced with anticipation. *"And I wait."*

What does he wait for?

"Your answer, Ilsaletta. What do you need most? With the Spirit Sword in your possession, you could possibly use it to carve me from your shadow and shunt me once more into

that blade. If it is protection that you need, then protection you shall have."

I set Stekkan's hand gently on his lap. It's welling with blood, but even so.

"One moment," I say to him before I turn and look at Vargaard, directly into his shadow eyes. "It is only ever you that I want."

I'm glad it's dark because when I turn back to Stekkan's hand, my cheeks are hot with embarrassment.

"*In your shadow or in your arms?*"

"In my arms. Always my arms. Did my kiss not make that clear?"

Vargaard's silence feels as flushed as my cheeks.

"You paused in stitching my hand to whisper sweet nothings to your lover?" Stekkan sounds annoyed.

"Can you see him still, even with the Tranquility Sword gone?" I ask, deflecting, as I clean the blood from his palm and start to stitch. He only needs one on this side, I think. Not much of the blade came through this far.

"He flickers in and out of sight," Stekkan says and then clears his throat. "I did not think that you'd be able to kiss him. That came as a surprise."

"It did to me as well," I say carefully as I turn his hand and begin to work on the back. The skin is thin here. It's hard to stitch without hurting something else.

"I admit to some jealousy," Stekkan says awkwardly.

I look up and raise an eyebrow at him. "Isn't that a little hypocritical?"

"I hardly see how," his tone is flippant which tells me he cares.

"Your heart belongs to Mercy and your body you have given to Jendaya," I say dryly as I tie a deft knot and move to a second stitch. He doesn't even flinch.

"My body has been given to many," he says with a shrug. "But I had grown used to thinking of you as mine."

"I'm not the one you married."

"Not as my wife," he scoffs. "As my monster hunter. It's a difficult thing to realize you are not solely at my disposal. I am your king now."

"Tell him he does not own you at all. Not in any sense."

I'm his friend.

"A friendship that is being tested with this talk."

I want to laugh at Vargaard's jealousy. Only he would be envious of Stekkan Falrune. I most certainly am not. I would not want to be wed to Jendaya.

"Nor I, but I envy him his ability to speak to you seductively."

There is nothing stopping you from doing the same.

He pauses, but eventually, he says, *"There is my honor, my Ilsaletta. I will not promise what I cannot yet give, nor will I take what is not mine to receive."*

I find this both touching and comforting.

I finish Stekkan's stitches and wrap his hand in the handkerchief to which he directs me. There are three in one pocket alone. I love how very Stekkan that is.

"So tell me, monster-hunter-who-I-must-share," Stekkan teases. "Whatever will we do now?"

CHAPTER TWENTY
NAKURAKI

I have tasted her love. After dreaming of her touch, the whisper of her breath, the warmth of her arms for night upon night. Her affections still warm my skin and my heart, like embers stoked for a long night. They are buried deep, but here they will remain radiant.

She is radiant. Beautiful in her blazing courage, captivating in her determination and faithfulness. Has ever there been a woman so true? She is very young. She is soft and vulnerable. And yet she does not cower or quake. She roars across the landscape like a cleansing wind.

Her father may fail her, her nation crumble under her feet, her compatriots all wash away, but I will not. Not when I was merely spirit and not now that the corporeal reaches for me. If what she truly needs is a man in flesh and bone, then I will skip and dance to meet the opportunity. I will dive into it to the very depths and fill my lungs with the purpose of it, daring it to choke me and drown me under the weight.

I am a bridegroom decked in flowers.

I am a hopeful merchant seeing his ship come in heavy laden with treasure.

Hopes cannot swell greater than mine have multiplied.

I flex my shadow hands and feel her skin still on the tips of my fingers. The curves of my arms feel her silhouette pressing into them. The length of my body has already committed her shape to memory. She is branded on the reality of my molten soul, laying her every feature into its hardening form. I have my substance in her desire, my phrasing in her love. Her heartbeat is the war drum that guides my feet and readies my hand for battle and in her eyes are all my many-layered dreams.

Perhaps, one day, I will be free to tell her all of this.

CHAPTER TWENTY-ONE

I draw in a long breath and sit with Stekkan by the candle. What little I can see of this place tells me we're on a path surrounded by waving palms. I can hear the sea. If there are other people, they make no light.

"We have three problems," I say calmly. "The first is the swords. Whoever wields them has the power to change everything for the worse. It could have been us. We could have joined them together, but now that Jendaya has destroyed some of them, that isn't an option. You said so yourself."

"And now we know for certain what we did not know before — that their Nakuraki can be freed to finally find release."

Release?

"Though my memories slip away, each one is stained through with that longing. I would have torn my own soul to pieces if it brought me the relief of death."

I'm still talking to Stekkan, as my mind turns over the deep sadness of Vargaard's words.

"The second problem is the gem. If it made the disease once, it can make it again."

"It also destroyed the swords," Stekkan muses, tapping his chin. His bird tucks her head under her wing to sleep. "It can destroy the rest. And perhaps, it can destroy the corricles and husks, too."

I nod. "It's a good idea in theory."

"Though how you would do it, I don't know. Run around touching them all like a child playing a game?"

"That could take a lifetime."

Stekkan clears his throat. "I'm a scholar, Ilsaletta, though you often forget it."

"I don't know why I do," I say dryly as Mercy hops down from Stekkan's shoulders and finds a place to cuddle up beside him, he tries to stroke her head and then frowns, forlorn.

"Yes, well, it's a failing of yours," he agrees, pouting. "Which is why you have yet to consult my opinion on the tome."

"You have an opinion?"

"I *did* read it, if you'll recall. And then I promptly raised you from the dead."

I feel myself flushing. I do owe him my life. "Thank you."

"And contrary to what you think, I actually am quite an excellent scholar and I retained most of it."

"You gave it to me to read," I say, stunned.

"Well, yes. Of course I did. We could hardly embark on

an adventure of philosophical theory and monster slaughter together unless we were both familiar with the material."

"I only managed to read part of it."

"Which is why," Stekkan says, nodding, eyeing me from over the candle, "I am reminding you that I read the rest. And there was an excellent bit of illumination at the part that illustrated how the green gem sucks in souls — or taints them. You'll recall that it was used to tuck your soul away quite neatly."

"I do recall," I say, feeling a little ill.

"The picture showed husks — smoke pouring from their cleft skulls — being sucked into the rent in the world. Into a sea of human bodies." He pauses and says, "so, I'd say there's a chance that the gem can indeed draw all these tainted souls back within the Sea of Souls — if we can only find the right way to use it."

Vargaard has been very silent as Stekkan explains this. I glance over at him.

"I'm sure you agree, Nakuraki." Stekkan regards Vargaard steadily.

My shadow guardian looks very worried. He runs a hand through his hair and attempts a reassuring smile for me. It only makes me more nervous.

"*The king is likely right,*" he says. But there is something he is not saying and I don't know what it is.

"What's the third thing, Ilsaletta?" Stekkan asks me. He's fussing with the bandage on his hand now and frowning.

"Third is your wife," I tell him.

"No, she's always the first problem," Stekkan says, slumping backward so he's lying on fallen palm fronds and slinging a forearm over his eyes. "She's always got to be the first problem."

"Well, she's nearly invincible as long as she has that gem," I say, thinking.

"And she knows it, too."

"I'm not entirely sure she's even human," Stekkan moans.

"Well you would know," I say, trying to think.

"You'd think so, but she's a slippery one. She could fool a man."

"I'm sure she could." My tone is absent as I think. "With the Spirit Sword we can carve our way in and out of the Sea of Shadows. Which means we could take the swords from those who possess them and fling them into the sea if we must."

"Better to destroy them," Vargaard says grimly. *"Who knows what power they might have within the sea."*

He makes a good point.

"You carved that big arc in the air with the Spirit Sword," Stekkan muses. "What were you thinking at the time?"

"Oh, I don't know." My tone is dry. "Something along the lines of 'Help, help, I'm going to die. Also, I have bird feathers in my face.'"

Stekkan snorts but then he sobers. "You wanted a place of safety, untouchable, far away, is that right?"

I shrug. "I didn't have time for clear thought, my liege."

"As your liege, I offer you a wager," Stekkan says, still

with his arm over his face. Is he planning to sleep here in the sand and fallen leaves with nothing but a single candle for comfort? I huddle into my coat, wrapping it around my knees and hugging them to my chest.

I used to take great comfort in my father's sea coat. Now it mocks me.

"Don't let every memory be tainted by his betrayal. It doesn't change who he once was to you."

Doesn't it?

"I don't have the time or inclination to gamble," I say as the wind stirs the palm trees, ruffling leaf on leaf.

"If this turns out to be a small island with less space on it than most Cragspear family farms and no clear way to escape it except using the sword, then you have to do the next thing my way." Stekkan's voice is firm.

"To be clear, we've done the last two things your way."

"I'm gambling on this because you wanted somewhere safe and untouchable. So the Spirit Sword opened the cut into an island. I bet that if you cut back into the Sea of Souls and then, say, thought really hard about how badly you wanted to be near the green gem, it would take you to it, too."

"That seems a bit like hand-waving to me. Magic rarely works how you think."

I agree with Vargaard. It seems a little too convenient.

"Then why didn't Jendaya just cut through to go retrieve you when she wanted you?" I ask.

That gives Stekkan pause. "I don't know."

"I suppose we could ask Haszinth."

"We could ... " he leaves the words hanging in the air.

"But neither of us wants to," I agree. "It wasn't in the book?"

"Can we talk about it in the morning? I'm exhausted and my hand hurts."

He's still gripping the hilt of the Mercy Sword, which is wise. I bite my lip. I want to talk about it now. But I, too, have not slept and there does not seem to be a threat nearby. I regard Stekkan for a long minute as I try to decide. Push him or give in?

"Let the man rest. He'll be more biddable in the morning and that will help our cause."

"If that's what you want," I say, unstrapping the Spirit Sword from my belt and setting it off to the side. I don't like sleeping in a strange space without a weapon close, but the idea of brushing the hilt in my sleep and having Haszinth suddenly at my throat is much worse.

"I will not let him attack you."

Even so.

"It is what I want," Stekkan says muzzily. "And if you decide in the night that you're too cold to be your usual prudish self, you're welcome to cuddle with me."

I'm speaking before I even hear Vargaard's growl. "You must love that wound in your hand if you're pushing my Vargaard to give you another."

"Vargaard," Stekkan says, musingly. It's like he's tasting a new food and isn't sure if he likes it. "*My* Vargaard. Is that what you call him?"

Vargaard says nothing but I hear his hum of approval in the back of my mind.

"Go to sleep, my king."

CHAPTER TWENTY-TWO

NAKURAKI

I do not think my Vali realizes what her king's revelation means. I do not think he does either. As they drift off to sleep, I become more and more certain that I must not tell them. If they do not know, then they cannot stop me, and if they cannot stop me, then they cannot blame themselves for what happens to me.

I was fool enough to believe I had a reprieve — that I could live as a man with the loves and delights that a man has. What a fool I am. There are no happy endings for the Nakuraki. There is nothing but guilt and shame and the debt we must repay.

I force down all those blind hopes and try to burn them from my heart. I was not made for happiness. I will not mourn its loss.

CHAPTER TWENTY-THREE

In the morning, Stekkan is proven right. We are on an island that is little more than a spit of land and a rocky outcropping. What I took to be a path is merely a place where the wind has carved away the sand between the palms. It takes me all of ten minutes to make my way entirely around and over the island. It's enough to confirm there is no boat or way to make one, no fresh water, nothing to eat — unless we are very clever at fishing with our hands — and no ships' sails in sight. We could be anywhere. At any time.

"*We are together,*" Vargaard says. "*And that will be enough.*"

I glance at him but he does not meet my eyes and he has not since I admitted what I need from him — what I want — that he leave this life of shadow and truly be mine.

If he doesn't want that, too, then perhaps I should take it back.

The sea breeze ripples my hair and the smell of salt

burns my nose. I'm sunk deep into the sensations when a new feeling ripples against my cheek and I gasp, turning my face to find Vargaard there. He is still mostly shadow, but there is a hint of opacity and color to him. His eyes are the palest blue. My breath catches in my throat. It is his kiss I've felt and he bites his lower lip now, screws up his face in concentration, and then his shadow hand finds mine and for just a moment, our hands squeeze each other and he lets out a shuddering gasp. I want to close my eyes to savor this touch, but I don't want to lose a moment of seeing him like this. Our gazes catch and I look long into his eyes and when he exhales and his hand is gone again, I still don't break our shared gaze.

"I want exactly what you want, Ilsaletta, my sun and stars. Do not doubt it for a moment."

I will not.

"I want to be a man of flesh and blood. To live my life with your hand in mine, your cares on my shoulders, your heart in my breast? What could be greater than that?"

Then why does he look so sad when it is clearly happening that way?

He does not answer me. Instead, he looks out to the sea and after a moment, I sigh and hurry back to my king. You can't squeeze answers from a stone. Or a shadow.

Stekkan is awake when I get back, unwinding his handkerchief and examining his hand. His stitches already need taking out, the Mercy Sword's healing properties are so strong. He holds his hand up to me and I sink into a squat and draw out my belt knife to pick the stitching free.

"You were right about the island," I say.

"Of course I was." He does not sound happy to be proven correct.

"Which means the only way we have to get off this island is Haszinth."

"Of course it is," he says, mouth twisting sourly. The morning sunlight spills over his brown skin and across his black hair in the most flattering way. Even here, dressed in stolen clothing, and streaked with dirt, he looks every inch the king he truly is.

"I'll draw the sword when we're done here and we can do whatever we must with him."

"What's the hurry?" Stekkan asks grimly. "There are no enemies here. In your moment of panic, you found us the one untouched place in the world."

"It's also blessedly untouched by food or water," I say wryly.

He laughs. It's a dark laugh with frayed edges. "But we could die in peace and leave these swords buried in the sand."

"That's a grim outlook. Besides, you know that these swords aren't safe here. They aren't safe anywhere."

He snorts, but not like he doesn't believe me, only like he can't believe that even his death will not be enough.

"What do you want, Stekkan?" I ask him gently. "I know what I want, but what do you want?"

He stares at me hard. "Oh, so now you know what you want, hmm? And is it life with your shadow as a living breathing man?" I say nothing but I'm sure my face flushes my answer. He sighs. "I want a useful task, Mercy on my shoulder, and the wind in my hair. Is that so much to ask?"

I smirk as I look at him. The wind is, indeed, ruffling his inky hair. Mercy bobs happily on his shoulder.

"Who would have thought that we had already found your heaven."

"I have found mine," Vargaard whispers in my ear and something warm fills my belly and starts to bubble up in my chest.

"And I want my wife dead," Stekkan says. "So dead that she can't be brought back."

"Five graves," Vargaard agrees.

"What did he say?" Stekkan asks, pointing the Mercy Sword at Vargaard so close that the blade almost nicks his shadow flesh.

"He says his people buried her kind in five graves to keep them from coming back."

"I like it. We'll do that, then."

It feels wrong to agree to that — too much like a plot to commit murder, but I nod anyway. Fine, five graves, it is.

"So now it's time to draw the Spirit Sword and ask our questions. And then we we tackle this trouble — first by disabling the swords, then the queen, and then the corricles — if we can," I say grimly. "Are you ready?"

"Yes," Vargaard says, *"Just turn so that you draw it in your shadow."*

I pick up the scabbard from where I left it in the sand and turn until my shadow falls over it.

"Wait," Stekkan says and I think he's going to object, but instead he hands me the Mercy Sword and steps to stand behind me. "You're still the monster hunter."

Fair enough.

I grip the Mercy Sword in my right hand and let my left hand touch the pommel of the Spirit Sword.

Haszinth is there before I can flinch, leaping out from the sword's shadow and the moment he coalesces, he leaps for my throat, only to be clawed back by Vargaard.

With a mental roar, my Nakuraki wrenches him backward, leaving little shreds of shadow behind. His face is screwed up in concentration. There's no sign of his spirit sword as he grapples, twisting his shadow body around Haszinth's bucking, screaming, gnarled one.

I open my mouth to ask him if he'll calm down so we can talk, but he rips free of Vargaard's grasp, lunging at me. His shadow hands close around my throat and my breath leaves me in a rush. I claw at hands I cannot grip and then I'm shaken violently and Haszinth is ripped free.

Vargaard twists him with a roar — literally twists him as one might wring a cloth. There are shreds of shadow everywhere, claws ripping into one shadow from the other.

Mercy screams from high above. I fall to my knees, still clutching my throat. I can't quite breathe. And then suddenly, they both puff out of existence. I'm left trembling, hands shaking hard, throat aching.

"I've got you," Stekkan says gently, helping me settle into the sand. "I've got you."

He sounds rattled as he takes the Spirit Sword from me and sheathes it, setting it to the side.

I finally gasp in a painful breath and let it out. Everything feels raw and painful. My head is pounding. I clutch the Mercy Sword tightly, desperate for the relief it brings.

"Now you know why I didn't want to draw that sword." Stekkan words are grim. I do know.

But it doesn't help us right now. We are still on an island in the middle of nowhere with no possible escape unless Haszinth comes back. And now we've lost Vargaard, too.

"Just rest, monster hunter," Stekkan says, putting my head onto his lap. "That's all we can do for now."

And if he sounds resigned, well I am certainly not. I am furious and anxious and devastated but I am not resigned.

And until this is over, I never will be.

CHAPTER TWENTY-FOUR

We wait. It is all there is for us to do. Stekkan reminisces a little about his childhood. I listen, but I would be lying if I said I am not also daydreaming about Vargaard and replaying our few shared kisses again and again in my mind. They are all the more precious for being few. All the more desirable for being nearly unobtainable.

"I loved ponies and dogs, riding, hunting, anything outdoors, and I loved music and dancing. When you are a duke, loving these things makes you very popular."

"I can only imagine." I let my eyes move over the waves, worrying my lip between my teeth.

"I've always been popular. Always been talented. Until one day I kissed a princess and discovered I had all the wrong talents. You can't dance away from death or whistle dogs to fight demons." His tone is maudlin.

"But now you are king," I say, staring out to the sea. "I would think those are good qualities in a king."

"I do not wish to be king," Stekkan says after a long

silence in which he rubs the stubble on his chin. "When all of this is over I do not want to reign and rule."

"We're unlikely to survive it all anyway," I remind him. It's not a very hopeful thought, but he seems to consider it a kindness. He pats me on the shoulder.

"And what about you?"

"What about me?"

"What will you do, monster hunter, when the monsters are slain and the world is free?"

His bird shrieks and leaps from his shoulder to attack a fly. She cannot catch it any more than the fly can catch her.

"I used to want to be a cartographer," I say quietly, staring at the clouds. I haven't considered this for a long time. Haven't realized — in the madness — how divorced we are now from any hopes or dreams we once had. "But I fear there will be no one to pay for the making of maps after this."

"Why not?" His brow furrows.

I snort bitterly. "If we cannot banish these turned, evil husks and corricles, Stekkan, there will be no life left for us. And if we do, then there will be one person left for every ten there used to be. We will have to work and work hard just to eat. Just to make cloth and mill wood. Just to produce candles and soap. It will be the work of generations to rebuild. There will not be writers of books, or makers of maps until my children's children's time, if that. Those are the benefits of a developed society where there are enough other people to do all the necessary things and so you can spare a few for extras."

"Maps don't seem like extras," Stekkan says. "Nor does music. Or writing."

"You only say that because you've never starved."

"I'm starving now," he scrubs his face miserably.

"And would you rather have a loaf of bread or a map of the island?" I ask.

"I'd rather have grim cold revenge. I'll die happy if I get that."

I make a noncommittal sound in the back of my throat.

"You don't believe me?"

"I know you too well," I say with a wry twist of my mouth. "You're a good man. Eventually, you'll learn wisdom and forgiveness instead of revenge."

He lifts a brow and now he is wry, too. "Like you have?"

"I've never claimed to be good."

He shakes his head. "And yet you are the best of anyone I've met. Honorable and true. I would call you a credit to your house, but your house is not worthy of you."

And after that, I cannot speak, both because of my raw throat and because he has choked me up with his lavish praise and all this talk of the futures we will not have.

We are both thirsty and hungry. The only one of us utterly unaffected is Mercy. She dives at tiny shadows, soars around us as if we are all playing a game, and shrieks her delight when Stekkan consents to tossing leaves and bits of stick for her to try to catch. It's adorable and just a little sad when they float through her spirit body.

I try more than once to draw the Spirit Sword. It comes out of the scabbard easily and slices through the air, but it does not tear into another reality and it does not bring back the Nakuraki. Unlike the Mercy Sword, the utility of this blade is bound up with its resident.

"Do you think he's winning," Stekkan asks eventually, biting his nails as he sits by the tiny driftwood fire I have made on the beach.

"He will win," I say with a confidence I do not feel. Whatever Vargaard deserves, though, it is not my skepticism. He will win. He must win.

"At least you chose a pretty place to die," Stekkan says, gesturing to the stars and the beach.

It *is* a pretty place. And my mouth is dry, my belly unhappy, my head light.

If we do not see the Nakuraki soon, we will most certainly die.

"When they get back, we need a plan," Stekkan says.

"Swords first," I say immediately. "Collect them in one spot. Then the gem. Destroy all the swords at once."

"In the Sea of Souls?" Stekkan asks, raising an eyebrow.

"Of course," I say. "The gem must stay there."

"And someone must stay with it," Stekkan says and his tone is testing me.

"I don't see why," I say, irritated.

But as the hours draw out, I do see why. He's exactly right. Someone will have to stay with the green gem in the spirit world because if it comes back with any of us into the living world, all of this will start again. And that person would be trapped there forever. It's a problem we won't be able to avoid and I know — without having to ask — that

Vargaard will want to be the one to do it. And I will have to think of some way to trick him into living, trick him so I can take his place. But I cannot think of how. I don't want to. A fate like that is unthinkable. Both for him, and for me.

The night seems to take a thousand years. Strange noises wake me so often I cannot tell if I sleep at all. Stekkan sleeps and as I lie awake I hear him murmur and even sob in his sleep and I try very hard not to think of what his wife might have done to him which leaves him both thirsty for revenge and broken when he doesn't realize anyone sees.

When day finally breaks again, I'm so relieved that I draw the Spirit Sword before Stekkan even wakes up.

My heart is in my throat. I fear the worst. My palms are so sweaty that I have to rub them on my trouser legs.

When Vargaard slips free first, I nearly collapse with relief, and then I see what he is holding. Haszinth kneels at his feet, his neck bound with cords of shadow. Vargaard holds those cords in a firm fist.

"Vargaard," I gasp, relieved. "You're alive."

"*I will always return to you, book girl. Death himself cannot keep us apart.*"

"*Bold words,*" Haszinth mutters.

But I hope this is true because the flicker of Vargaard's smile fills me with joy in a way that nothing else can. I don't care, suddenly, that there will be no cartography for me, no future like I'd once hoped for. Vargaard is the only future that I need.

"*He shouldn't have been able to attack you,*" Vargaard

tells me. He looks slightly worried. *"Somehow the power of the swords is crumbling."*

"Vali or no Vali, she is not worthy of my dedication," Haszinth says. His words are laced with barbs.

He clearly is not submitting to me just because I hold his sword. Perhaps the swords fed off each other and with two gone, it weakens the others.

"Perhaps." Vargaard seems unconvinced. *"But he is ours to direct, for now. And I suggest we act promptly."*

"I will never be yours," Haszinth says and his teeth snap off the end of his words like he wishes he were biting into me.

"Good," I say aloud, ignoring Haszinth. "We need to track down the other swords, collect them, and bring them to wherever Jendaya is keeping the Green Gem so that we might destroy them. That is the only option we have left. To cripple her power, take her magic and undo the armies she has unleashed upon the world."

"Then wake the king. We must not delay, lest I lose my grip upon this hostage."

"Can you fight with him as your hostage?" I ask, hesitating.

Vargaard hesitates with me. "I don't know."

I shake Stekkan awake, by my eyes are on Vargaard and Haszinth. If our time is limited, then we need to begin immediately. The last swords must be collected. No matter what the danger might be.

"Oh," Stekkan says with a yawn when he sees the shadows watching him. "The gang's all here. Have you found a new beloved, shadow bodyguard? You're holding him so tenderly."

"*No.*" Vargaard's single-word answer holds an edge and Stekkan must be able to read his lips for he answers back.

"Pity. Come on Mercy, let's fly. Close your eyes, Ilsaletta, swing that sword, and let's get off this terrible lonely island. Your king commands it."

And as little as I like being commanded by Stekkan, I follow this command to the letter.

CHAPTER TWENTY-FIVE

"If you're serious about this endeavor," Vargaard says, tightening the noose around Haszinth's neck until he gags, *"then you must be ready to fight the moment the sword carves the air. Both of you."*

I give Stekkan a look as I ready the Mercy Sword. "Vargaard says we must be ready to fight immediately."

I swallow, gathering my emotions. Readying myself to listen to all of Vargaard's instructions.

"You do the fighting, monster hunter. I will do the reigning," Stekkan says, drawing himself up and opening one arm up in a gesture that signals Mercy to float down and rest just over his shoulder.

"Maybe you should handle the Spirit Sword so that I can fight, then," I suggest.

"No," Vargaard says, shaking his head so that Stekkan can understand, too. *I"f you sheathe the sword and then redraw it, I will have to battle Haszinth again and with a*

new soul in control of the sword, who knows how the balance might shift."

"Then we go in like this," I say, drawing a huge breath and readying my double swords.

"Exactly as I like it," Stekkan agrees.

"*Be ready for my commands. Act instantly. We will be at a disadvantage.*"

"Yes," I agree.

And then I brace myself, slash the Spirit Sword in the air and think of the Sea of Souls.

Haszinth screams like I've slit his actual throat, but the tear opens and we spill into the Sea. We are not on the bone boat this time. We are in the thick of the Sea. Stekkan screams from behind me and his hands tighten around my waist as we are buffeted by the crowd of the dead and shoved hard to the side. My ears fill with the wails of the despairing. There is no room for us to shove into. We are pushed, instead, into more souls.

I can hardly breathe.

"*Slash the sword again! I can't hold them off for long!*"

It's not until he speaks that I realize Vargaard is pushing the crowd of souls away from me, clearing just enough space in front of me to swing the Spirit Sword.

I grit my teeth and think hard about a Nakuraki stuck in a sword. Wisdom was one of the swords. I think of a Nakuraki who was so full of wisdom he was refined down and it was all that was left of him. And then I slash through the air and as the slash is still opening, Stekkan yells and shoves me from behind and through the slash.

We emerge in chaos. I suspect a few souls have tumbled out with us, though I cannot tell in this madness. My heart is immediately in my throat.

"To your left!" I think it's Vargaard screaming, but to my surprise, it's Stekkan. I jam the hilt of the Spirit Sword at him.

"Take this," I gasp as I spin, letting go of the sword before I even feel him take it. I need both hands on the Mercy Sword and by the time I finish the spin, I'm glad that I do.

"One step to the right. Now."

I obey immediately and a pike runs through the space where I stood only a moment ago, jabbing right between Stekkan and me. I hear his strangled cry, but I don't have time to react like that. My attacker's guard is open with that thrust. I take advantage, jamming my sword up and under his pike. He shudders, blood streaming from his mouth and down an Istraverdan uniform. I'd feel worse, except there is smoke streaming from a fissure in his face in a purple plume. He's a husk, not a man.

"Mind your rear! Quick, spin to the right, keep the blade high!"

I respond, trying to take in details as I move. The slash in the air is closed and it's just Stekkan and Vargaard and me. Vargaard is spinning me to thrust my blade into the side of a soldier who is still turning to see what the chaos is behind his orange-plumed back. We're squeezed into their ranks, a knot of fury in the middle of ordered military lines. I can't see past the press of bodies.

"Duck! Press to the right. Harder!"

I follow Vargaard's instructions precisely as he whirls around me, his shadow sword slashing out to carve our enemies away from every side. Stekkan's hand grips my shoulder tightly. He's pressed as closely as he can be to my body as we slide through the wake of Vargaard's destruction.

"Sword up! Get ready to burst forward and run."

"Get ready to run!" I call to Stekkan and then Vargaard tosses two creatures out of the way and an opening clears.

"Go! Quickly!"

I run.

We burst into the opening, chests heaving. We're between two groups, I realize. Two — armies? If you can call this second group an army. It's more of a huddle of beleaguered vagrants. Those not openly bleeding and swathed in filthy bandages are still so dirty that it's hard to see men beneath the grime. They are huddled on a hilltop, weapons at the ready, a hasty barricade of fallen logs their only defense.

"Look around you so we can assess."

The army at my back is ten times the size. All turned to husks, for the most part, though a few corricles float their spirit creatures forward. The husks — almost to a man — roar defiance at the tiny huddle. Behind their ranks, a man with a high cockade hat holds a sword above his head, waving it and yelling something that I'm sure is an encouragement to the troops or something but I can't hear the actual words from here. He's their leader. And that is the sword we need.

"We're in Istraverda," Stekkan gasps, pointing in the distance to where twin domed towers rise. "That's the Twin Gate. The entrance to the country from Cragspear. I rode this way in my aunt's entourage once. We were touring the great gardens of the seven nations."

"How lovely for you," I say but I don't see lovely towers. I see smoke rising from where they've been set alight. I see bodies strewn in crumpled heaps across the plain to this barren hill that's mostly tumbled rocks with that one tiny cluster of trees.

Stekkan is still explaining, "These huddled defenders are dressed in the garb of their army — just like the attackers. If I had to guess, I would say that the small group is the last of the defenders of the gate — they wouldn't even have had time to turn yet — and the main force are those recruited by Jendaya."

"Good guesses," I say. But even knowing what we're dealing with doesn't help. We need a plan and the army we just escaped is plunging in our direction.

That destroyed Tranquility Sword and its power of invisibility would be very nice to have right now.

"Do not fret. We have another way. A fast, brutal way. We don't have to do it. We can still flee."

It will only get worse from here as these swords end up at the heart of power of every nation surrounding us. Then it won't just be armies we must slash through but bodyguards of corricles well-organized and with plans.

We must do this his fast brutal way.

"Okay. Tell Stekkan to hold on tight."

"We're going back in," I tell Stekkan, even though my

hands are already trembling — and not just with fear. The earth itself is shaking as the vast army marches toward us.

"You've got to be kidding me."

"Vargaard says to hang on tight."

"To what, precisely?" His objection is nearly lost as Vargaard plunges forward.

"Run! Run hard. Blade up!"

I get my blade up as the army crashes into us and by rights it should sweep me up into the air, let me hit the ground with a smack, and then trample me until I'm nothing but a corpse flattened in the mud. But it does not.

I gasp as Vargaard hits their charge with a charge of his own. I may be the only one to hear his shadow roar, but it fills my ears and fills me with courage.

"Do not stop. If you stop, you make yourself a target."

As if we're not a target now.

His blade snakes in front of me, skewering a monster and I must step promptly over the monster's writhing body to keep going, but Vargaard is right. As he slashes and hacks and throws and disables, his advantage is momentum and we must not lose ours. I shove my sword into any openings I see, hoping I'm helping, but mostly just panicked and trying to hold on to enough courage to keep putting one foot in front of the other without tripping on a corpse or a man about to be one.

"Mercy! Mercy! See how the mighty fall."

It's almost a comfort to hear Mercy shrieking. I know without knowing how that as long as she is here, Stekkan lives, though I also know it by his hand on my shoulder —

a hand that grips so hard that I'm dead sure it's leaving bruises. He's taking Vargaard's orders seriously.

I spare a glance for him and see his face in a rictus of fear, but to my surprise, he also has the spirit blade in his other hand and Haszinth is leaping out from it, defending Stekkan's life even as his mouth makes words that I am sure are curses. It seems Vargaard does not have to fight him again if it is Stekkan wielding the blade.

"What is he saying?" I gasp as I leap over a fallen man whose writhing smoke is trying to catch my ankles. I refuse to allow that.

"He's cursing me," Stekkan says through gritted teeth. "Calling on all his gods to torture and slay my whole family."

"Have you told him that they already have?" I ask, having to yell over the maelstrom.

"I don't dare distract him," Stekkan says, gasping as he runs right into me when I pause to try to figure out how to get past two still-thrashing bodies Vargaard has laid in my path. "His defense is better than the alternative."

"Poor Stekkan. First one monster hunter and then another and both thorny problems."

"Yes," he says tightly, but he can't say more because a man breaks through while Vargaard is distracted.

I crouch, sword up, but he ducks under my guard, grabs me by the hair, and drags my feet out from under me in a single yank. I can't get my sword up. It feels like it's trapped on something. He flings me to the ground and raises a sword gleaming above me.

I see my death in the blade.

I suck in a gasp. Trying to move but I'm pinned under his boot.

And then a sword thrusts through his chest. It's oddly clean for something so close and personal. As if it's almost an accident.

He shudders and his blade drops to the side. And then he's shoved backward and his boot is off my chest long enough for me to claw up through the bodies around me and find my heaving feet.

My eyes shoot up, looking for threats. I see Stekkan, looking down at his own hands in horror, pretty mouth spread wide in a terrible grimace as he views the man he just murdered for me. Behind him, a furious Haszinth slides his shadow blade through a man's throat who was an inch from decapitating Stekkan before spinning to take down two more in a single blow. He keeps a swath carved around the king. A disorderly reaper, systematically cutting a pattern known only to himself.

"*Ilsaletta!*"

I spin to see Vargaard doing the same on the other side. He risks a single look at me, his eyes shot through with fear. I can tell he wants to say something but doesn't know what to say. He settles for an order.

"*Don't stop moving.*"

I stumble back to my feet, grab Stekkan's stunned hand, and pull him after me.

"Thank you," I gasp to him. "Thank you for my life."

"I ... I ..."

It's fine that he's stunned. He saved me. Now, I save him.

I can tell he's back there, buzzing with a thousand Stekkan thoughts. I keep him close to me, grasping his hand tightly.

I can't tell how time is passing. Moments seem to take hours, so perhaps it's only been a few moments or perhaps it's an entire day, but all of a sudden Vargaard's arms are moving twice as quickly and then real smoke creatures are shooting toward us and it takes all four of us — yes, Haszinth is helping too, since he's bound to Stekkan — to fight off these raging smoke creatures, shove through their ranks, and finally come face to face with the cluster on horses.

Vargaard doesn't even hesitate. He cuts the horse off at the legs — a nasty move and one I wouldn't condone except that now the man with the sword — whoever he is — is down at our level. His Nakuraki is tangling with Vargaard — and it gives me the chance to leap and smash the Mercy Sword into his chest. It doesn't even have to be a good strike — I know that already. Not when it has all the extra pain the Mercy Sword has been saving up ready to shove into my victim. It hits him like plunging his head under a waterfall and while he's fighting and thrashing from the force of it, I lean over his screaming horse and snatch his sword out of his hand.

The nobleman's Nakuraki freezes, turning his head to me at the same second that Vargaard smacks him in his shadow head with a fist, and he's stunned and wavering, but he hits me with something so hard and fast that it makes me stumble, too.

"Ilsaletta!" Vargaard shouts, clearly upset, but I'm not

physically hurt. He hasn't hit my body, he's hit my mind. The Wisdom Sword, clearly, has latched on to me and cut through into my mind to give me the exact answer I need.

"*When you leap back into the Sea of Souls,*" this Naku-raki says, and it's like he's shouting it directly into my brain "*— PULL!*"

And I don't wait to see what happens next as Vargaard spins and charges toward me and catches a second nobleman on the edge of this shadowy blade right before the man plunges something into my back. He is chest to chest with me for a heartbeat, breathing past my ear, arm extended around me, and in the violence of the moment he is flesh and blood.

"Cut us through," I call to Stekkan, my senses popping with acknowledgment of Vargaard against me, of the heat of the battle, of the horse screaming just under me, and the men all around, and Stekkan, wild-eyed and gasping. "Cut a doorway and when you do it, pull as hard as you can."

"What in the Seas of Souls does that mean?" Stekkan gasps as Haszinth shoots past him to rip an attacker literally to pieces.

"Pull all these evil monsters in with us!"

"Why would I want to do that?" he asks, his voice reaching a register so high that I think I'd be hard-pressed to reach it with him.

"So that we don't leave them *here!*"

He makes a cry that's half squalling complaint and half desperation and then Mercy lands on his head like a descending angel granting him peace, and he twists up his mouth in fury, eye blazing at me in accusation, and flicks his sword in an arc.

Reality tears with the sound of ripped fabric and without even moving we're sucked into the gap and dragged into the Sea of Souls.

CHAPTER TWENTY-SIX

Stekkan is no fool. Emotional, yes. Easily frustrated, yes. But he's not a fool.

We land in the Sea, tumbling like tiny shells whirling in the curl of an ocean wave and hundreds of other souls are sucked in with us. They tumble, too. And tumble, and tumble in a wash of helpless fury. And I have no idea if Stekkan closes the gap behind us. I can't see. Both my hands are full of swords. To my relief, one of his hands reaches out and grabs my belt and it keeps us together as we tumble.

By now one or both of us should have been skewered on a blade — killed entirely by accident before we even land — but Stekkan swishes his sword again and we fall into a new gap to wherever he has sent us.

Us — and about five other souls.

I land on my bottom — hard so that I feel the jarring go right up through my bones — onto a marble floor. Vargaard is already moving in front of me, feet braced as he grabs and tosses one, two, three souls back into the sea like a farm wife dealing with troublesome chickens.

Stekkan landed a little better than I and he's in a crouch, hands up. As Vargaard throws the last soul back through, Stekkan flicks his blade, closes the gap, and tosses the Spirit Sword away from him. It clatters on the marble floor and bounces off a stone hearth. The sound of this violence rings in the air for long moments after the sword settles.

I gasp, trying to still my shaking limbs, and stay where I am, staring at a huffing Stekkan who is staring at me.

"I think I can do without being dropped into any battlefields in the future," he says, white-faced and wild. His hands are shaking so hard that they seem to be rattling his jaw. He doesn't seem ten years older than me right now. He seems exactly as young as I am.

"So can I," I agree. "But you did it. You sucked that army into the sea with us."

He doesn't answer and I don't think he's proud of his accomplishment. He shoves his face in his hands and lets himself collapse to the floor while I pick myself up and stand.

"He's rattled from the battle. It happens to new recruits and they're better equipped than he is."

This is almost compassion coming from Vargaard. What does he think of all this?

"I think it suggests that if you really collect all the swords and destroy them then you can also suck those who have turned into husks and corricles directly into the Sea of Souls

and if you do that and remove the Scourge of the Stolen Heights from play, then you will have saved all the world."

He stands before me, looking tense despite the fact that he's just given me the most hope we've had all this time. His eyes are locked on mine and he seems almost entirely solid.

"Do you really think so?" I ask, not because I think he's wrong. I just want to hear it again. Hope springs wild and bright inside me. We could ... we could save all the innocents who escaped? We could give them a real chance of picking back up and starting again? We could make a world that doesn't need monster hunters? We could do all of that.

Vargaard is nodding. *"I think so. Yes. If we time everything perfectly. If we have the will and we use the Spirit Sword aptly before it is finally destroyed ... yes, we can do it."*

My eyes prick and I take in a shuddering breath. It's almost too much. Too much to hope for, to wish for, to have. I can't bear it. I blink back tears as the emotions saw through me — isn't hope worse than despair sometimes? — and look around me, trying to find something trivial to replace the roiling joy that threatens to leave me with my face in my hands just like Stekkan.

"What is this place?" I ask aloud, turning to finally look.

I visited the palace in Swordheart one time. This place is built to a similar level of luxury and beauty, though it is built differently. We're in a massive room — as big as the dining room in my father's house in Saltfast. It's formed of a pale golden marble shot through with ripples of metallic, shining gold flecks. Pillars hold up a high dome ceiling where someone has fancifully painted sunrise clouds.

Huge doors — twice my height — are formed of lattice and inlaid with stained glass panels in shades of yellow and frosted white. They're ajar and a drift of leaves and blossoms — dead now — wash into the room with the breeze. A massive bed on a platform is still made, layered in quilts, and furs, and curtained with filmy curtains like summer clouds. The hearth is laid as if any moment now someone might swoop in and close the door, sweep the leaves away and kindle the flame.

This room clearly was for someone very important. A king, perhaps.

One door opens to what must be a bathing area. I see a large tub sitting at the ready. Another is open into a place hung with furs and garments on hooks. A line of boots long enough to equip an entire complement on one of my father's ships stands under them on the floor.

Oil paintings in vibrant hues depicting landscapes and horses — quite a few of horses, actually — line the walls and the room is full of gilded stand mirrors, small tables scattered with books, towering shelves with more books than even my father's library had, and a slanted drawing desk with stacks of schematics that I think might be parts of the human body. All these things fill the expansive room, as do two settees, a fine tufted rug, a collection of lutes in one corner on fancy rosewood stands, and several brocaded chairs.

I turn my back on the luxury and hurry to the door. I must understand the lay of the land.

I glance at Vargaard, who nods sharply. He agrees that we must get more information. My second glance goes to the Wisdom Nakuraki. He has not introduced himself or said anything else. He paces beside me, clad in a robe, but otherwise, he does not look old or young, fit or lazy, beautiful or ugly. He simply is.

He raises his eyebrows at me and then says, *"If you want to suck in every soul tainted by the Scourge of Stolen Heights then one of you will have to stay within the Sea of Souls to complete the task. There will be no hopping back and forth like little frogs, or you'll quickly find them all hopping with you."*

I feel my face flush. I did not want to have to speak of this to Vargaard yet.

"I'll sleep then, until you need me."

The Wisdom Nakuraki is gone before I even start to slip his sword into my belt loop.

"He spoke to you," Vargaard says, his gaze piercing mine.

I look away sharply. My hope of a moment ago is already making me ill now. I have still not found a way to trick my Vargaard into living while I accept death. I still have not found how I will resign myself to it in the first place. All I know is that I don't want him giving himself up for me and I know he will the moment that he realizes what is happening here, and that there's only one way this ends with any of the good still alive. It will take a sacrifice. Mine or his. And I do not think it is right that it should be his.

I twist my hands together and look into the distance but I don't take in any details. My eyes are misty with unshed tears and my breathing is harsh.

"Look at me, Ilsaletta."

"He will sleep until we need him again," I say, offering half the truth and trying to hide the hitch in my voice as I slip out the door and try to look across the vast garden beneath the terrace. A hundred varieties of flowers bloom. I see three fountains just from here and a pond with trees on either side whose drooping branches spill their leaves into the water. It's idyllic and lovely with rolling hills beyond and beauty in every direction.

But just past those hills, there's a glow in the sky and a dark cloud. And in the glow I see the occasional fresh pillar of black smoke drifting upward.

It's no surprise that whoever lived in this villa abandoned it. The chaos in the distance will be here soon enough. We've dropped from one scene of madness to another. Just as we will again and again unless we end this and perhaps I am only a soft bookish girl who fell madly in love with her own shadow. Perhaps I am last of my line, twisting a different way than my father or the father before him, but I will take on this task. I will do what must be done. I think of the duchess fleeing Seabring with a carriage full of orphans and I blink back tears and I know what I must do.

"You have not answered. What has the Wisdom Sword said?"

I dare not tell Vargaard. He will stop me because he loves me. And I love him which is why I can't let that happen.

"It's my house," Stekkan says, suddenly, stepping from

behind me to join me at the railing, looking out over the garden. "My suites."

I look over my shoulder. His?

"For how long have they been yours?" I say because I don't know what else to say. Did he inherit this huge estate, perhaps? It's big enough to hold ten of my father's house and I can see stables in the distance and smaller buildings of many kinds — all built from golden marble as if it is as easy to acquire as wattle and daub.

"For ... always. I grew up in those rooms as a child and then refurnished them when I came to majority. Did you not see the paintings of horses?"

I look at him for a while until he blushes.

"These are my family's country estates. I told you that Ghregoiren was beautiful. You can see that from here, can you not? She's enough to steal your breath every morning. Of course, we have a home in the capital, also."

"Of course," I say hollowly. "Your family doesn't seem to be at home."

"No." His words are quiet. "Were there anyone here — any at all — there would not be leaves on my bedroom floor." He looks at the glowing sky. "Perhaps they left when someone lit the capital on fire. Or perhaps sooner."

I swallow then. This is not good.

"I took us here because it was the first safe place I could think of," he says. "But now, I see it is not safe at all. I have no idea where else to go. The island again, perhaps."

"There was no food on the island," I say and he nods sadly.

Which is how we find ourselves making our way to his abandoned kitchens. There are apples in a bowl — still without spots — and cheese in the larder, though the milk spilled on the floor from a smashed jug has turned. A few dried sausages hang from the rafters. Overall, it makes for what passes for a feast now. We tear into it — but not in the kitchens or the great dining room where chairs are left pulled out or toppled completely and a half-eaten breakfast is abandoned.

We eat, instead, in Stekkan's room and on his bed.

"They must have gotten out," I say. "During breakfast. They might have been warned."

My words are hollow and I know it. They could just as likely have scattered after the plague reached them, but there are no husks wandering around trying to kill us, so I still think my conclusion is possible.

"Perhaps," he says, unconvinced.

Vargaard is very quiet as we finish and then as we both take turns bathing with cold water we haul from the kitchens and dressing in Stekkan's wardrobe. His clothing is large and loose on me, but it is clean. I choose his drabbest clothes — which are still too fine by half — and I leave my father's coat behind. And if I feel a whiff of regret it is only because this coat used to mean safety and hope to me and now all of that is empty ashes in my mouth.

"*You don't have to leave it,*" Vargaard says.

But I do.

Stekkan has not bothered going for subtlety. He has chosen a tangerine jacket over a brilliant turquoise waist-coat and a pair of cream breeches beneath them both with high leather boots.

It's only after we dress that he leads me to the armory. It's been pilfered — but not completely. And there he finds me a harness that will sheathe two swords across my back and a belt with two sheathes there, too. He finds himself a fresh belt with double scabbards. We look ridiculous with all these empty scabbards hanging everywhere but it's a practical choice nonetheless. We shuffle our weapons to their new homes and then make our way back to his rooms in silence.

"You are planning to destroy all the swords, suck every one of these tainted people into the Sea of Souls and then stay there yourself, aren't you?" Vargaard asks me eventually with an edge of violence to his mental voice and I won't answer him. Because if he knows, what will he do?

We reach Stekkan's bedroom and he sits on the edge of the bed before shucking off his boots and belts. He keeps his clothing on, though. We both know, without saying it, that we might have to leap again at a moment's notice. This interlude of food and clean clothing is but a stolen gasp in the middle of the battle.

"Tomorrow we'll hunt more swords, Monster Hunter," he tells me and now he's not meeting my eye, either, not even when Mercy hops up onto my shoulder and coos in my ear. "But first I need rest. And so do you. Bar the door and let me sleep and if you're sane enough to sleep, then join me in this bed."

He mistakes my hesitation for maidenly modesty.

Is it not?

"I swear I will not so much as touch you," Stekkan says as he flings himself back into the pillows, tangles one of the quilts around himself, and turns his back to me. "There are other rooms in the house, of course, but do you truly want to be separate if we are set upon in the night?"

I do not. It's better to stay close together.

Our swords are set in their sheaths beside the bed. Stekkan put the Spirit Sword into a sheath with his hand covered in three gloves as if one was not enough to prevent loosing Haszinth.

Our adventures today have somehow sucked up all the daylight hours. The sun is sinking on the horizon. I clench my jaw and tap my knee in indecision.

"If you are planning such madness, then you owe me the truth."

Vargaard is suddenly before me, kneeling on the floor facing where I sit on the edge of the other side of the bed from where Stekkan is trying to sleep. His expression is wrung as if he is in torment but I can't relieve it. I dare not tell Vargaard what I am planning. Not that I know, but even this determination of mine will be too much for him. He will feel the need to protect me from myself and it will doom him. And haven't I already demanded everything from him? I will not ask for his eternal soul, too.

"Please. Do not hide your heart from me, book girl. I have given all of mine to you."

I look away.

"Please. Don't look away."

I swallow.

His mental voice sounds like it's shredding when he speaks next and he sounds young. Nearly as young as he looks, for once. Nearly as young as me.

"Please, please, my darling Vali. Please do not blow so cold."

And how is anyone supposed to turn her back on that? So I turn to him and I reach out my hands only to feel them pass through him once again.

Vargaard.

"Yes," he sighs into my mental words. *"Please, please don't make this plan, Ilsaletta, or at least don't make it without me."*

But I can't do this with him. He'd never allow me to sacrifice myself.

"Of course not. I am your protector — until death and beyond. If one of us is to fall, it will be me."

I shake my head violently. This is exactly what I was trying to prevent.

"Don't you see?" His tone is so pleading, the look in his eyes so sincere. *"Don't you see, Ilsaletta, that you can have a future. If we end the swords and Jendaya and the gem and suck every husk and corricle into the Sea of Souls then you can keep living and you can rebuild the world alongside the king of your nation."*

I'm already shaking my head again.

"As his friend, I am not asking you to marry him anymore."

But why would I want to do any of this without Vargaard?

"Without me, perhaps, but also for *me, because there is nothing I want more than your future. Won't you give me this one thing that is in your power to give?"*

Now he was just playing dirty.

"Please?"

He leans in, pressing kisses I cannot feel to my cheeks and forehead and mouth and I'm consumed with the desire to hold him, to kiss him back, to give him everything. This is what I will lose when I encase myself in the Sea of Souls and make him go back to the real world. It hurts just to admit it to myself. I want to keep him. He's all I want to keep from this whole world. And it would be the worst of cruelties to do it to him.

"The only thing I've ever wanted you to give me is you safe."

But that's not what I want.

"What do you want?" He asks, his hands running down the sides of my face without touching, his lips leaning in and kissing me without me feeling it. He stops and looks into my eyes with anguished longing. *"What?"*

And it's possible that I'm blinking back tears when I whisper, "All I've ever wanted is you."

"Yes, lovely, fine," Stekkan says in a muffled voice from under a pillow he's thrown over his head. "You can have me. All of me. If you'll just shut up and stop fawning over your own shadow for long enough to get some sleep, I will be your plaything for as long as I live."

"In your dreams, Stekkan," I snap.

"Yes. That's what I'm *begging* for!"

He yanks the pillow off his face and sits up long enough to grab my shoulder and pull me down onto the mattress. I yelp as I fall back, but I can't deny the softness of the bed is glorious, and combined with my terrible exhaustion, I don't even want to move.

Vargaard, doesn't know this. He launches himself toward Stekkan, but Stekkan just throws a pillow through Vargaard's shadow form.

"I'm not trying to fight you, Nakuraki, and I'm not trying to sully your Vali. I just want sleep, and you won't stop talking."

Vargaard pauses and Stekkan nods and falls back into the pillows with his back to me again. "Go to sleep, Ilsaletta. Let your shadow cuddle you if you must, but go to sleep and let me dream, and in the morning we'll go do terrifying things again, just like you love."

He drags a pillow back over his face — there are so many — and all I want to do is obey, but I'm fighting with Vargaard and he deserves my attention. He deserves ...

I realize suddenly that he has tucked his shadow between Stekkan and me.

"The king might be right. Sleep, my Vali. And I will protect you from all threats. Even the threat of an unwanted cuddle from your sovereign."

Which, given that this is Stekkan, seems pretty likely. I don't even have enough energy to laugh at my own joke. I drift and before I can even kick my boots off, I am asleep.

CHAPTER TWENTY-SEVEN

I sneak out before Stekkan is awake and find a place on the wide steps outside the stained glass window. We can't stay here for long. In the distance, I see figures moving on the hills, and to see them from this far away must mean there are hundreds of them. These will be the people pouring from the burning Ghregoiren capital. Some are perhaps innocents, fleeing the maelstrom. But most of those hundreds or even thousands that I am seeing are people turned and warped by evil. Not their first encounter with evil, simply the evil of their own hearts finally manifesting and either being controlled by them to create greater horrors, or taking the reins and spurring them into a maddened frenzy.

I sit with my back to the dawn, my legs crossed in front of me, and when Vargaard sits in my shadow and mirrors me, I see he understands what I want here.

"I don't want to fight with you," I say quietly.

There's a light breeze stirring my hair and whirling it

around my face. It ruffles Vargaard's shadow hair and sets a little painful burst through my chest. He's slowly becoming flesh again just in time to want to give it all up.

"It's not a fight." He shakes his head. *"Our bond is not threatened, our loyalty not affected. We simply don't agree."*

His smile is losing the ageless depths it used to have, looking younger, brighter.

"What do you want, Vargaard? When all this is over, if we win ..."

"We will win."

"If we win, what will you do after all of this? When there are no more monsters to fight?"

"There are always monsters." His face is set with stubborn determination.

I shake my head.

"That can't be all you want. To hunt monsters. To kill them."

He's looking at me steadily. *"You know what I want."*

"You can't only want me," I say thickly. It's sweet, it is. But this can't be all there is to him. "You can't want only to be with me and nothing else — or you truly will be my shadow even if you become a man. I can't live with that, Vargaard. I won't allow that to be all that you are."

His expression turns sad, but he just watches me.

"This is why you think you need to stay in the Sea of Souls. Because there's no future out here for you."

He shakes his head and draws in a sigh and when he speaks, it comes out as a voice and I'm so stunned I miss the first few words as my breath hitches in my chest.

"My sun and stars, I do not at all wish to be forever

adrift in the Sea of Souls, nor do I wish to cross over with the Fisher King and lose forever my sight and taste of you. But I will not lose you that way, either. I do not choose that path, but if the choice is you or me then let it be me. I do not thirst for a life beyond you, but that does not make me less a man, it makes me a man boiled down to the smallest thing he once was, concentrated to a single point."

"Mercy," I gasp, and I can't help but lean forward until my forehead nearly touches his shadow one and his expression softens.

"Yes. Me, and the sword, and the bird. That's what we are in the end."

"And what do you want?" I press gently. I swear I can feel his forehead against mine and the feeling of it carves a warm channel in my heart.

"That's all I want, Ilsaletta. A taste of mercy. I don't even deserve that, but it's all I long for beyond you. Mercy for me, that the endless cycle of my suffering might be over. Mercy for you, that you will escape this terrible snare. Mercy for your people who are groaning under the weight of all the evil of the world. Is it too little a thing that this is my ambition? Too narrow of a desire for a man? Then I do not deserve a future, I fear, for it is all I want."

"And if you get it, what then?" I can smell his breath. It smells of oranges. I shiver slightly.

"Then we will think about how to spread it further afield. But I dare not dream beyond the impossible hopes I already have. My audacity, even now, is too great, and when my dreamings shatter and rain down on my head they shall pierce me straight through."

And I think I finally understand now. He's a broken man, battered by time and loss. It's cruel to ask him to dream pretty rainbow dreams when all he's known is the harsh eye of the sun.

I reach across and cup his cheek with my hand — almost touching it. "That's fine. That's just fine."

And when his eyes meet mine they're grateful and I'm swept away by this gratitude for the tiniest shred of mercy. I'm not worthy. I never was.

"I won't leave you adrift out there alone," I whisper, and I say it like a vow because if he's going to do this, then I am, too, whether he likes it or not.

His eyes are devastated, but he lets me reach for his hand and we both gasp when I find it's solid enough to hold.

I close my eyes for just a moment and lean into the warm comfort of its solidity. It's a gift — a terrible, wonderful gift for which I'm not worthy. I just want to cling to it forever. I know he cannot save me from what is to come. And yet, holding his hand makes me feel as though he can.

When I open my eyes, his are on the horizon. They swim with unshed tears just like mine do.

"I think we must act again soon, my book girl, time runs short."

It's still a marvel to hear his rumbling baritone voice with my ears and not just in my mind.

He is right, however. The forms in the distance are rushing ever closer to us. I must focus.

"I think I should consult the Wisdom Sword. The

Nakuraki within knew about pulling tainted souls into the sea, perhaps he knows a way to pull the swords in, too."

Vargaard does not seem convinced, but he also does not move or shift as I draw out the Wisdom Sword and lay it bare over my knees.

The Nakuraki within leaps to life and stands in the shadow of the blade until he sees we are sitting and then he folds himself neatly into a crosslegged position on the cold hard marble of the terrace as if he is one of us.

"Do you have a name?" I ask him gently.

"Wisdom has no name, understanding no moniker," he says which isn't terribly helpful. I glance at Vargaard to be sure he can hear this, so I'm looking at his face when the Nakuraki continues. *"I am spirit and shadow. I have not made the fool's bargain as this one has."*

Vargaard's jaw clenches and a tremor of fear grips me.

"Fools bargain?" My eyes shoot straight back to the Wisdom Nakuraki.

"Nothing comes from nothing. And yet this one has bargained for a corporeal body once more. He receives his wish, he ties himself to a mortal woman."

Vargaard nods sharply. He has known this all along.

"I am mortal with her," he agrees.

I do not think the Wisdom Nakuraki laughs. He does not now, but I draw from this that he does not ever. Because he looks at Vargaard for a long beat, his eyes narrowing as if he is working out a puzzle that strikes him as odd, and then he says.

"And where are you getting your mortal life from, fool of a Nakuraki?"

When Vargaard is silent, gaze turning inward, the other Nakuraki shakes his head.

"You get it from her, obviously. You have linked yourself to her life, her body's strength. Every ounce you take to make yourself solid comes from her."

Vargaard's gaze springs back to his.

"Yes," the Wisdom Nakuraki says hollowly. *"By the time your transformation is complete, you will drain her utterly and both of you will fall to shadow and ash."*

My heart is in my throat. I think my hands might be shaking.

"Don't cry," Vargaard's words seem rough and panicked. "Don't cry, my Ilsaletta."

He reaches out and his arms are firm enough to hold me and he draws me in and tucks me into his lap, cradling my face against his chest with the gentleness of a man cradling a dying bird. But I am not crying for myself. *This* embrace. This one chance to be held while I cry might be the only one we ever have and it is being bought with our two lives. The misery of it, the awful snatching of this understanding shreds my heart and rips me to pieces.

"There's a way to reverse it, surely," Vargaard says hoarsely.

"Of course," the Nakuraki says. *"Give yourself to the Sea of Souls before the transformation is complete. Let it eat away this physical body as it eats away all things, and let your soul remain within it and the girl will be as she was before."*

"No," I gasp at the same moment that Vargaard says, "Yes, of course."

And he doesn't sound hopeless or despairing, just

relieved. He kisses my brow and runs gentle fingers through my hair and down my back as if he can caress my sorrows away but they are building. I choke on a sob. In this one moment, all these hopes I'd been clinging to are ripped away in a breath.

I can't keep him and live. Not as a man I can hold, and not even as a spirit protecting me. And I'm realizing that yes, all he wants is me, but also all I want is him. And I'm going to lose him entirely. We've been running out of time all along.

I look up and catch my Vargaard's eye and he's smiling down at me gently, bravely, but my jaw trembles terribly as tears drip from it.

"This is not what I wanted for you." My voice is thick.

"It is not a thing that can be fought." His words are gentle, as if speaking to a child.

"Then I will go with you."

He's already shaking his head. "I would die before I allowed that. You will live my Ilsaletta. Such a beautiful name. And you will live a good and full life."

"Not without you," I protest.

"I have no regrets." I can feel it costs him to say this to me, though he does it with a smile. "I do not regret this end in any way. To have known you even a little while, to have been given this time to love you — I have been given a mercy from heaven that was never mine to take."

"Your time runs out," the Wisdom Nakuraki says, looking at the hills and I wonder if only yesterday he was giving balanced but opposite advice to our enemies.

"Can the other Nakuraki and their swords be sucked

into the Sea of Souls like the corricles and husks were?" Vargaard asks the Wisdom Sword.

I should be a better woman. I should be the one asking. I should wipe my tears and crawl out of Vargaard's lap and be asking these questions myself but I feel as though someone has cut me in two and is asking me to live that way.

"Of course. With intention and the Spirit Sword."

"So the duke ... the king ... can simply carve a slit in reality to them, and what ... will them to come to himself?"

"If he is in full control of his wants and desires," the Nakuraki says. *"But you will not move much else that way. Only things that belong in the Sea already — evil creatures, and all tainted by the twistings of the Scourge of Stolen Heights."*

Vargaard is nodding. His warm arms flex around me and the feeling is lovely. I'm trying to memorize it. To hold on for just one more moment.

The moment is broken when a throat is cleared and we all twist to see Stekkan leaning against the wall of his own house, one ankle crossed over the other — the picture of ease. But his face is freshly shaven, his hair arranged and he is wearing fresh clothing. For reasons undiscernible to me, he is dressed entirely in shades of cream and white from his fitted trousers and vest to the billowing shirt beneath and the close rabbit-lined coat.

"Having a nice little chat without me?" he asks coldly, raising an eyebrow. There is some kind of emotion bubbling just under his frosty exterior. I don't know what it is, only that it is a strong one and he is hiding it from us.

"Am I not to be part of this next leg of the journey then? Me and the Spirit Sword?"

"Of course you're part of things, Stekkan," I say, but his bitter gaze is what finally makes me pull myself together, climb out of Vargaard's embrace, and rise to my feet, Wisdom Sword in my hand rather than on my lap now.

I sniffle, but I don't let go of Vargaard's hand. If I have so short a time, I will not lose a single opportunity to tell him with my touch that he is wanted, treasured, more sweet to me than life.

"So, you're a man now, are you?" Stekkan says to Vargaard and even now that he has a voice, Vargaard ignores the jab, saying nothing. "And is this the part before we go out and do something stupid where we look around our little circle of three —" Mercy squawks from his shoulder and he corrects quickly, "— four, and congratulate ourselves at how far we've come and all that we've accomplished? Do we remind ourselves that we are now the dearest of friends, the only ones each other has, a family of misfits and fools?"

"If you want us to, Stekkan," I say carefully, not sure what he's doing.

"Shall I tell you both that your love touches my sour heart and I want nothing more than to see your star-crossed love succeed?"

"Is that what you want?"

Vargaard still has said nothing. He watches Stekkan as if expecting an attack at any moment.

"No," Stekkan says and then swallows visibly. "I don't.

So you shouldn't have been expecting it. But you should be grateful. My family lived here and clearly, they are long gone. My wife is my new family and it is her murder we're all plotting. So. My family is maybe something you don't want to be."

"*Mercy!*" His macaw cries at that. "*Mercy. Mercy. Mercy.*"

"Yes," he agrees dryly. "Have mercy on all of us. Gather your things, Ilsaletta. If we're going to destroy the last swords and send my wife to the next life, then we have a busy day ahead of us. And I don't much want to wait for it to get busier."

He gestures to the figures in the distance who are becoming clearer with every passing moment.

"I'll take that other sword with me. I have a few questions of my own."

The Wisdom Sword Nakuraki looks at us grimly as Stekkan snatches the hilt from my hand and then he turns and strides back into the house.

"*What you do, do quickly,*" the Wisdom Nakuraki says, and I don't think there is a trace of sadness in his eyes, though surely he must know that we plan to destroy him, too.

CHAPTER TWENTY-EIGHT

I prepare quickly — washing, drinking, and snatching up a water skin to take with me. A brief perusal of the rooms nearest Stekkan's garners me a more feminine set of clothes, though they are a little too short and wide in the hips, the trousers move well enough and the jacket, bustier, and shirt fit far better than Stekkan's do and were chosen by someone far more able to stomach a normal color palette.

Vargaard follows me everywhere I go, but he isn't entirely in my shadow. Sometimes, he strays out of it and seeing that sends icicles of fear stabbing into my heart. He's growing more human by the moment. He's growing more vulnerable.

He catches me around the waist after I dress and I can't help but glance at the bed — not Stekkan's bed, obviously — but he's already shaking his head. We don't have time for that and even if we did, I have a feeling that Vargaard would never agree without taking more vows first.

"Ilsaletta," he whispers instead, as he kisses me reverently — and yes, chastely — on the cheeks and eyelids. It makes my heart flutter despite the circumstances. "Whatever comes next, I need you to know, that for me this has all been worth it. I would have chosen no other path."

And I have to really fight to reply because my throat is thick. I wish I could have found a better path for him. One that made him free and whole.

"I love you, too," I say simply. It will have to be enough.

We stand together for only a heartbeat — a single breath where I get to run my hands over his glorious arms and back, and then we break apart because we both know we're running on borrowed time.

I sheathe the Mercy Sword and I find a place on the terrace at the same moment that Stekkan returns. His formerly neat hair is wild as if he's run his hands through it several times. He shoves the Wisdom Sword at me.

"I have my answers," is all he says as he shakes his head at me and then he looks me right in the eyes as if it's only the two of us and he says, "Once this begins we can't stop until the end. No breaks. No retreats. No hesitation. I need your word on that. To the very end."

He needs *my* word? Stekkan who is rarely brave and never so certain needs *my* word that I will not falter?

"Of course," I say and I'm surprised to hear Vargaard say, "My word, King of Cragspear."

Stekkan nods us to us grimly.

"I'll draw in the last of the swords and then immediately bring my wife in afterward, and we shall hope she has kept her secret source of evil on her person so that we can dispose of all of them at once."

"All at once?" I say, and yes I am afraid, but I'm also eager. This nightmare that never ends could reach a conclusion. Suddenly. At once. The very thought of it fills me with hunger.

To my surprise, Vargaard takes my hand for just a moment and then he says, "When the moment comes, King of Cragspear, I shall take the burden."

I'm already shaking my head but I know it's no use. He knows — and I know — that he will disintegrate out here. He cannot remain in the world of the living. All that remains is for me to decide to join him in the world of the dead. And of course I will, won't I?

"I beg of you, do not make this choice."

But it is my choice and not his. I clench my jaw tightly and Stekkan yawns.

"I'll bear your request in mind, monster hunter," he says to Vargaard, as if it is my shadow guardian asking him for a favor rather than offering up his life. "And now, we must be quick. We must gather together all that we need and act decisively so that our enemies have no warning of our plans and no way to escape."

We nod our agreement and Stekkan swallows, looking a little green, and I did not expect to be doubly surprised by him, but he draws the Spirit Sword and does not flinch when a raging Haszinth flings himself out of the blade's shadow, snarling and snapping.

"He's forced to serve me," Stekkan says to me dully.

"He could fight you if you held his sword, but I am by rights his king as well as his Vali and he cannot deny me."

He shrugs and then — casually, almost haphazardly — he swings his blade and rips a tear into the fabric of reality and white light blares across our vision as we step into the Sea of Shadows.

I'm braced for what comes next, but I'm not ready. Especially not when Stekkan takes a knee right in front of me, bows his head, and *pulls* and every husk and corricle from the landscape behind us is drawn in as if on fast-moving winches, tugged against both will and credibility, straight through that gap and with us — onto the deck of the bone ship.

I look up even as my eyes are widening and I see him there at the helm — my father, ragged and skeletal. A gasp escapes my lips as his mouth curves into a rictus. His body has been ... picked away, bit by bit. It is as if he has been at the bottom of the ocean and eaten by fish.

My gasp catches in my chest but Vargaard is yelling at me to pay attention and draw my sword. I bring the Mercy Sword out as my shadow guardian — more flesh than shadow now — tosses a husk away from me — one who was moments away from tearing out my throat. I grip the Mercy Sword hard and breathe as his instructions pour over me. I'm moving from the moment they begin.

Left. Dodge to the right. Down to one knee, sword up! And spin now to the left. Sword neck height and ... slash! That's good.

His instructions have led me right to where I can bowl over two enemies and he's already barking new orders, dancing the same way that he's led me as he pushes and pulls, hacks and slashes.

"If you open those slashes near the rail, maybe it won't put them on the ship next time," he calls to Stekkan who nods back as if the pair of them are compatriots.

I shake my head, surprised. Especially when Stekkan darts to the ship's rail and he slashes hard, muttering to himself and then catching a sword in a scabbard as it flies through the rip to him. He jams the full sheath into his belt quickly and then begins his fight again as if nothing has happened. He pulls through the slash and thousands — yes, thousands of mutated bodies come ripping through, stretching the edges of the rip like pulling too large a rock through a slash in a sheet or — and I hate to say it this way, but like a sack full of maggots, where one cuts a tiny hole and maggots wiggle and bulge and fall, fall, fall out. Just like that, these souls are so many that they crowd out everything else and just pour wriggling and disgusting through the slash. They are terrible mutated smoke husks, their faces split open and hideous and with them, fall the corricles, fighting against this with every scrap of energy their smoke creatures can generate. No amount of fighting and struggling can keep them from pouring into the sea. I think some of them are dressed as the guards of the Hexipluris. He must have had the sword Stekkan drew through the slash.

They fall too quickly to catch the deck of the ship, so we sail alone on a white ship of bones in a white, white ocean, with the mist of madness all around us while my friend pours more and more mangled bodies into an already chock full sea.

Stekkan is already slashing a second cut into reality while the first is still open and streaming. A second sword flies into his hand and his mouth curls into a snarl of determination. He flings the sword at me and I fumble but catch it. The scabbard falls off but I keep my hold on the grip as the sheath falls away and a Nakuraki leaps from the heap.

Stekkan is out of control. He's slashing and slashing and now bodies aren't just falling into the sea, they're falling onto the ship and raining down on us from above.

"It's too much for him. It's breaking his mind."

My father is bellowing from the tiller as the added weight makes the boat yaw and lean.

"Ilsaletta!" Vargaard's cry sends me spinning. He's guarding my back, but blood streams down his arm, dripping red, red on a deck of white. He's too human. Already his clothing is pocked and ripped.

I leap to his aid, slashing with the Mercy Sword in one hand and this new sword in the other.

"For the lost!" the new Nakuraki screams and with his scream, I feel a sudden jolt of fearlessness that propels me forward.

I have courage. I have it flowing through me like a waterfall. But it's not going to matter. The souls are flooding over the decks, the ship is leaning to the side. This is way out of control.

My father bellows through the chaos.

"I care not for the madness you bring, daughter, but

unless you wish to wreck us upon the shoals, you'd best move starboard!"

I know the difference between port and starboard. And I know my father well enough to heed his advice on this.

"Stekkan," I yell, "the other way! We have to move the other way!"

The press of bodies is too great. They push at us from every side.

Even in human form, Vargaard is fast. He meets my eyes as often as he can, pressing courage through his gaze as he hacks and whirls. I fight, too, as he has taught me but I do not have centuries of practice. I must settle for stabbing at any opportunity I see. I sheathe the Mercy Sword and fight only with the new Courage Sword. I dare not let it down, not when this Nakuraki boldly darts back and forth into the fray protecting both Vargaard and me.

I do not deserve these Nakuraki.

No one does.

"If you did not find slavery troubling, I would worry far more."

Vargaard catches my eye as he says that and then spins into a double twist that drags five husks into each other.

The edges of his clothing are more tattered than they were before. He is bleeding freely. I feel a pang deep in my heart. We are not losing, and yet we are at the same time.

But our ship is righted. It's leveling off, riding rough over the screaming writhing souls beneath.

Somehow, we are all still here.

Stekkan is screaming at the top of his lungs, but some of his slashes are empty now and closing, and others, though still overflowing with roiling souls, are slowing down.

"Get this madness off my rig!" Admiral Redtide roars, and I realize that even in this short span of time he's disintegrated more. Just as Vargaard will break apart, so my father's physical form can't stay firm in a world comprised of only spirits.

Vargaard is bleeding badly. His eyes catch mine, distressed when he sees my intention. He's caught where he is, clearing the last of the husks away.

Stekkan's scream has amplified and he's untouched — totally ignored by the terrible souls swirling around us, but my father is here still and I can't help it, I can't. I stumble forward and I hold his withering gaze and I say, "Why?"

"Sometimes, Ilsaletta," he says, and if he has an expression I can't even see it, never mind read it. "Sometimes the tide simply turns against you."

And I want to ask what that means, but there's no time. Mercy dives at me screaming her name, and then she grabs a hunk of my hair and pulls me back to where Stekkan is still screaming and screaming as if he is personally birthing the entire world. My Vargaard has cleared the decks and is rushing to the side of my king, heaving, bleeding, swaying slightly.

With every moment we spend here, time is running out, and Vargaard is running out with it.

"Fear not for me, beloved. I am with you until the end." He does not sound despairing. He sounds firm and steady.

"Stekkan," I say desperately. "We have the swords. We need the green gem."

But he isn't listening. He's just screaming and screaming as if he is being tortured and then abruptly, he slashes the air behind us over the rail of the ship, cross-hatching his slashes so that they are wider and deeper, and then he abruptly stops screaming.

And this time when he pulls, Farrakki fall through his great cross-hatched gate first and then a myriad of twisted humans pours out like the tilting of a wagon of grain into the sea and the ship tilts upward so the deck is nearly perpendicular as we crest this great wave of wailing souls.

Stekkan heaves, bowing over the side as he clutches the rail and vomits into the sea, and then, swallowing and sweating he turns toward us. The boat heaves just like our king, up over the crest of the sea. It smacks down hard on the other side of the wave, the force of what we just crossed propelling it forward.

My father is cursing at the helm. I hear my name specifically, which is nice, there's nothing like being in hell and then also cursed to a worse fate than that.

But the slash my unsteady king has made in reality is opening up.

"Be ready," Stekkan gasps drawing and then shoving the other sword he had gathered toward me. I have to drop the Mercy Sword to sheathe this new one and then pick it up again quickly, so I barely see my Courage Nakuraki spring to place himself between the gap and my body. As I fumble with my grip, Vargaard catches my eye one last time.

"Courage, my Vali," he says in my mind. *"To the last drop of my blood, I will defend you."*

And I want that to be full of security and love, but all I feel is fear because if he gives the last drop of his blood, then he will give what I value most — himself. I do not want him to give away — as if it is not precious! — that which I love most.

I gasp in a shuddering breath.

"What can I do to make you stay?" I beg of him, and I see something in him break and weep though his face remains steady.

I'm making it worse. With my love and desperation, I'm making it worse. And I don't know what to do. How do you comfort someone when you cannot offer them even the hope of tomorrow? When you cannot promise them even yourself because that is what they most want to avoid.

I've done it all wrong and I don't know how to make it right.

"I'm sorry," I say because I don't know what else to say. "I'm so sorry. Do whatever you must."

He pauses, a look of love and torment rippling across his features and then he smiles gently and catches a fistful of my hair, drawing me into a kiss that's sweet and kind but desperate and hungry all at once. It leaves us both gasping.

And his eyes are liquid blue and beautiful as the sky away from this white, terrible place, and his shuddering breath between real, human lips is precious. The subtle tightening and loosening of his features as a thousand thoughts roll through his mind are my treasure. But if you cling to your treasure, it will slip through your fingers. I cannot keep him. I do not know why I ever thought I could.

"What do you need?" I whisper.

"Mercy," he says and his word shudders out. "Live for me, my Ilsaletta."

"I will try," I agree and the agreement hollows me, makes my mouth and throat dry and thick. I do not want to live without him. I don't.

"Please," he says and he presses his forehead to mine. "I woke to you as a worshipper to a goddess. Let me die for you as a man for a woman."

I choke down a sob but he's shaking his head as he keeps his grip tangled into my hair. His voice trembles.

"Let me love you to the end. It is an end I am not worthy of. A death I would have begged for had I known it was possible."

"Vargaard," I whisper, but he cuts off my whisper with a kiss so passionate and thorough that it fills my heart and tangles all through my grief, leaving me equal parts agony and love, despair and tenderness.

"I recognize that goodbyes are very important," a sick-sounding Stekkan says, "but if you're about done, I'm losing my grip and I need to finish this."

And when we both look over at him, breaking out of our embrace, he nods once, firmly and then he focuses on the slash he made in front of him and his face twists up as the slash begins to heave and shudder and out of it flies a pair of furious corricles and a dazzling woman with long golden curls and eyes full of hate.

"Greetings, beloved," Stekkan says, and then promptly vomits a second time.

CHAPTER TWENTY-NINE

No one should ever underestimate Jendaya, Queen of Cragspear, but unless they have a half dozen armies of their own and a terrible ancient artifact bent on human destruction then they aren't really at her level.

Jendaya may very well be as terrified to be sucked out of the rip in reality as everyone else is — just as her corricle guards who, well-dressed though they are, tumbled out the rip like seaweed in a departing tide — but if she is, she shows no sign of it.

Her heeled boots step smartly out to the bone-encrusted ship, her head — crowned — is held high, and in one hand she carries the scepter of Cragspear. In the other, she carries the Scourge of the Stolen Heights — the green gem. She looks every inch a reigning queen and her unicorn bursts forth before her like a shield.

"There you are, wayward husband," she says in a bored voice, as if he has just returned from getting her a drink at a country dance. "And you've brought your rebel friends with you. Marvelous. It certainly simplifies things to keep you all in one place."

Stekkan shakes himself, rising to his full height and lifting the blade of his sword.

"Oh, and you've gone and collected the whole set," Jendaya says, running her eyes over his sword with apparent boredom. "Or at least, as many as I left you to find. You know they can't defeat me if there aren't seven of them, right? If your aim is to dispose of them, though, then don't let me stop you. I think they're a liability, to be honest. Any fool can wave a sword around."

She directs a look at me as if to emphasize her words, but when her gaze hits mine, her unicorn shoots out toward me.

I lift my sword in defense and the Courage Nakuraki leaps toward the specter, ready to defend me at the cost of his own life. I am ready, too. This may all be happening with a suddenness that disorients me, but it is what we have come for — to destroy the swords and Jendaya all at once, and if the reality of it makes my heart beat double-time and my vision feels fuzzy, then that is a small price to pay for what we are doing here.

"*Sword up! Lunge forward!*" Vargaard directs me even as the Courage Nakuraki engages the unicorn, but everything seems to happen at once.

Jendaya lifts the Scourge of the Stolen Heights, laughing. A light bursts from the gem and the sword in my hand shatters into fragments, the Nakuraki bursting into dust as the unicorn leaps right through it. Pain stabs my palm and wrist where shattered metal has splintered and shredded my left hand. I release my grip but it does not ease the blinding, thought-scattering pain.

Vargaard slips between the unicorn and me, but he's late, his human reflexes too slow compared to his shadow self. The unicorn horn sinks into his shoulder as he shreds it with his shadow sword. His *wuff* of pain cuts deep to my heart.

I hear a sliding sound and glance to the side in time to see Stekkan sheathe the Spirit Sword — insanity! — and leap toward Jendaya.

Her corricles are still in chaos as they pick themselves up from where they have tumbled at her feet. Her scepter is too delicate to make an adequate weapon and her other hand is full of the gem. And yet she barely flinches as her husband bowls her over, hands wrapping around her throat.

I gasp, but my hand is in agonizing pain, even with the Mercy Sword gripped in the other. Sweat beads on my forehead and my breath comes quickly, thoughts scrambled.

Vargaard lurches just in front of me as the unicorn rips its smoke horn free of his shoulder. He shudders but his wounded arm still moves faster than my whole one. He backhands the unicorn and then flips the backhand into an arcing slice that splits its smoke head from its body and my hopes rise just in time to be dashed as this one smoke creature is replaced by six more.

They roll over Vargaard, snapping and ripping,

covering him so fully that I cannot see more than tiny glimpses of him. A scream catches in my throat. I dare not stab at them or I will catch him, too. I run, instead, towards the nearest corricle, blade up, and it's only because it's the Mercy Sword that I manage to damage him at all.

With only one working hand, I do not wield the sword well and pain clouds my vision. I strike the man with the flat of the blade — a blow that should do little more than sting, but the sword pushes out all the pain its taken in, and it's taking more by the moment with my hand injured. It shoves all of that into my victim and he goes stiff, falling backward and tumbling over the railing of the ship.

One down.

But when I spin, two more are coming for me and a third is ripping Stekkan from Jendaya. I can't even see Vargaard under the mass of smoke creatures.

"Stop fretting for me and fight!"

It's good advice. And I'm glad he's still alive to give it.

I wrench my eyes and heart from him and lift my blade back up, stumbling forward just as Stekkan yells, "Ilsa!"

The green gem flashes through the air and my heart leaps into my chest. It tumbles toward me and if I miss this catch we'll lose it entirely, over the side and into the Sea of Souls, and who knows what the desperate bodiless creatures below would do with such power. I drop the hilt of the Mercy Sword and I leap, catching the gem with both my good and my ruined hand. I draw the Wisdom sword from the sheath on my back and plunge it in, feeling the wrenching of the Nakuraki as he departs.

I'm not done. The other sword Stekkan collected — the Generosity Sword, I think, is next. I draw it and plunge it in, trying to quell the curiosity in me that longs to see what this sword can do before it's gone. It's wrong to keep slaves. Curiosity is no excuse.

I did not even see this Nakuraki manifest once, but now it is gone, dust and ashes, its long-dead spirit fleeing into the sea. I grip the gem tightly, ignoring the terrible pain in my ruined hand as the first corricle rushes toward me. I'm not enough to push him back. Not enough.

And then suddenly Vargaard is there, bleeding, dragging one leg, and still shaking off smoke creatures as he leaps, flattening the corricle to the deck. I'm just drawing in a shuddering breath when a hand tightens around my throat.

"You have something of mine, little mouse," Jendaya breathes in my ear. "And I plan to take it back."

I twist in her grip just enough to see Stekkan on the ground beside her. Two of her corricles hold him down while he clutches his face. Someone has slashed him right across the eye, leaving a harsh cut over the eyebrow and across the forehead on a diagonal and down one cheek. If he's kept his eye, he's lucky. He's sucking in little raspy half-sobs.

I clutch the gem hard in my bad fist, fighting off the pain, but the Mercy Sword is ripped from my grasp as two corricles push me down to my knees, too.

Vargaard is fighting the rest, flagging, but working hard. He's everywhere at once, blocking one blow, leaping right over a sweep to his legs, spinning so his offhand clips another attacker across the ear, and then landing, only to have to dodge a blow that almost carves straight through his midsection. He's breathing hard — harder than I think he should be — and the very edge of his jaw is rough as if something has been gnawing on it. So quickly — too quickly — this place is eating his physical body.

I squirm, fighting the grip on my shoulders, but I can't kick free.

A distraught Mercy circles overhead screaming her own name. Her cry echoes across the deck of the boat and is lost in the raging sounds of the sea.

"Don't let them escape again," Jendaya says off-hand, and just like that, one of the corricles smacks Stekkan hard with the hilt of his sword.

My king goes down in a heap, blood flowing freely from his head, body boneless. His hands fall free and I see his ruined face. He almost looks like a blooming husk this way. The idea twists my stomach. Mercy settles on his back, worriedly pecking at him.

But I can't wait to watch more. I dodge a strike to my head and squirm hard until something strikes me in the face.

"*Ilsaletta!*" Vargaard cries, distressed. And I want to help him, but I've lost my sword and I can't pull myself free from the grip of the corricles. The ones who had held Stekkan down are moving to intercept Vargaard, who — though bleeding heavily, one arm hanging limp at his side — has defeated all comers. His guard is almost too slow as he tries to leap between them. He's not fast enough. They make him dance and dance hard, huffing as they fight.

I gasp as another blade sinks into him — this time into the meat of his leg, but he plucks it out and throws it away and the corricle with it.

"Hold on, my sun, my stars!"

His voice in my mind is desperate. He cannot afford to spare me a glance. And then pain blossoms in my back and the corricles holding me drop me to rush at Vargaard. I try to stand to catch them, to hold them back, but the pain is too great. I crumple to the deck.

I can hardly seem to break my own fall. Reality flickers in and out, dark then light again and Jendaya's face swims into view.

"A knife in the back seems fitting, don't you think?" she says, clawing at my shredded hand.

But I can't let her have what it holds. I can't give it up. What is it again?

My vision narrows. My heartbeat is uneven. I don't know. I don't know what I'm doing anymore.

Everything is narrowing to little flashes.

Jendaya's face is close to mine.

Vargaard is in my mind. *"I'm coming."*

Mercy screams something unintelligible.

Jendaya's face screws up in concentration as she pries at my hand and then another face grows large behind her, a face I know like my own.

"Tides change," my father rasps out. "And then they change back."

His hands wrap around Jendaya's throat. Her loud curse is cut off as her eyes widen.

And then they stumble backward.

Hit the rail of the ship.

Topple over the edge and seem to almost balance there for a moment, his arms wrapped around her flailing body. And then my father's eye catches mine and I swear I see him wink as they fall over the edge and into the sea.

CHAPTER THIRTY

My heart is in my throat. I try to pull myself up but nothing is working, not hands or feet over even lips. I'm shaking all over, teeth rattling together.

The ship lists and I roll, smacking right into Stekkan.

His eye opens and his bird screams, tugging at him, and just like that he's being helped to his feet, swaying and all I see are his boots.

"She needs the sword. Where is it?" Vargaard demands, and then he's there, lifting me into his arms, face desperate, blood pouring from multiple wounds on his head and in his chest. I feel a wrench as the dagger is drawn from my back and he tugs me in close.

"Ilsaletta, my beauty, my sun," he says through bloody lips, and his words are broken and crumbling just like him. It takes a heartbeat and a shuddering breath before I realize they're made ragged by sobs.

I try to say his name but I can't form it, can't find it.

Someone takes the green gem from my hand gently and

hot tears splash on my face. Warm fingers take my hands and wrap them around the hilt of a sword. It seems to ease something within me so I don't have to clench my teeth quite so hard around my shaking but it's still so overwhelming that I can't speak, can't think.

I feel and then see Vargaard's kisses on my face and forehead and I've never seen him like this. He's fully flesh, his cheeks flushed and healthy, his carved features beautiful in the stark bright light. His dark hair is in disarray and his skin marred with blood and bruising, but he's beautiful and far, far too young, barely older than I am. His lower lip trembles and his bright eyes are swimming with tears.

"Don't go, Ilsaletta. Don't leave this body. Hold on. The Mercy Sword will help you, I swear it, just hold on. Please, precious girl. Please." He's begging me in that gorgeous velvet voice of his and I want to obey. When have I not obeyed and been saved because of it? Never. He has held my hand and my life in his palm since we met and he holds it now.

He kisses me just once on the lips, he's trembling so badly he can barely press them together. And I know this is goodbye. I know it, and I don't want to say goodbye. I want to hold onto him. I try to, but my hands won't hold him, my lips won't form the words.

"Take her," he rasps out and pushes me into Stekkan's arms and I feel as I'm transferred from one warm strong pair of arms to another and now the worried face I look into is Stekkan's. His smile is sickly as he takes me in his arms.

"Shh. All will be well, monster hunter."

He tilts slightly as he carves a slash through the air with the Spirit Sword. And when he moves me slightly I catch a glimpse of Vargaard standing there — not his normal straight-spined self, but with shoulders slumping and a grim expression on his hollow face as if he has been stripped of everything, even life itself. There is a terrible wound in his belly that he's trying to hold with one hand. It's already soaked everything beneath his waist with blood. And I want to tell him to come with us, not to stay here. He doesn't need to stay. We'll leave the gem on the ship. Who will ever find it there?

"Stay close," Stekkan commands him. "When we step through the gap, I'll give you the sword. You'll know what to do."

My Vargaard is nodding and there's tension in the air between these two as if they're making vows I can't hear.

No. No. No. This isn't right. I hate it. I feel my eyes welling with tears but I can't find the words. I can't do more than rasp out my beloved shadow guardian's name.

"Vargaard."

I hear the choking sob that pulls from him but I don't see him because Stekkan has turned and is stepping out through the slash he's cut in reality, leaving the Sea of Souls forever.

He leans down and whispers to me.

"Ilsaletta, look at me." I see him only through my tears. His face wobbles and runs. "What's about to happen was always the way it had to be."

But it didn't! It didn't. It could have been another way.

It should have been. And I hate that I can't fight this. That I'm helpless before my own heartbreak.

"It's well, Ilsaletta," Vargaard assures me aloud and he sounds far away. I think maybe he's lost his ability to speak to me in my mind. The loss freezes me to the core. And I know he's trying to be strong for me, but I hear the tremor in his voice as he says, "All is well with me. Go with Stekkan now, and *live*, my love. Live for me."

And now I get to see him because Stekkan is turning, hitching me in his arms so my rolling head is better cradled by his shoulder. He moves as though he's trying to shift the sword in his other hand. Vargaard reaches an open hand, ready to take it.

And when he does the slash will seal and he'll be gone. I'll never see him again. And I don't even get to say thank you. I don't even get to say goodbye.

And then, without warning, Stekkan lunges forward, and his blade slices neatly through Vargaard's chest, parting his living flesh and thrusting through it. He grunts. Staggers. His eyes are full of betrayal and then a look of shock and horror floods his features.

I want to scream but I'm not sure I do. I claw weakly at the arms holding me but they only grip me tighter.

I blink. And suddenly the blade is not in my Vargaard's chest anymore. The hilt is in his hand and the gem is in the other and he smiles suddenly. An odd smile that I've seen before, but never on him. And Mercy settles on his shoulder.

Mercy?

And then Vargaard plunges the Spirit Sword into the

gem, winks at me, and the blade crumbles to ash and the gap begins to close.

And I'm shuddering with sobs when he calls to me in *Stekkan's* voice, "I always fancied sailing the seas. And I could never leave Mercy, you know."

The bird settles happily on the shoulder of Vargaard — Stekkan? — and his hand rests on her feathers. She leans into the caress and the last thing I see is the pair of them sailing away into the great Sea of Souls. And the last thing I hear is her cry of, "Mercy!"

But I think that I see the net of the Fisher King coming down and I'm nearly certain I see the edge of it scoop them up before a flash of light steals the last sight of them away.

My head lolls and I finally catch a glimpse of he who holds me, and the face is the face of Stekkan, but the voice, when he speaks, is the wondering voice of Vargaard.

"Ilsaletta?" he asks, as if somehow he doesn't know who I am. As if I am the one who the Spirit Sword plucked from one body and placed within another.

"Vargaard?" I manage to gasp, before the pain finally claws up and sweeps me away.

CHAPTER THIRTY-ONE
NAKURAKI

Millenia have not been enough to forget my mistakes nor purge my past. But redemption is possible. I know that now.

I saw it in the sacrifice of another.

I see it in the look in my beloved's eyes every morning.

I know it, for it guides my steps and holds my heart.

I asked for mercy once.

But I was given so much more.

EPILOGUE

Sometimes when I sit at the desk that was once my father's and pour over maps drawn by his own hands, I wonder what he was thinking when he chose to tip the scales and drag our queen down into the sea with him. Was it love that turned his heart? And if it was, why not sooner?

I think that, perhaps, it was up to him in that moment. Not up to Vargaard, or Stekkan, or me. We were too busy fighting for our lives. And it wasn't up to Jendaya who thought she'd already won. It was up to him.

Had he taken her side, I would be gone and she would rule.

Had he chosen her, the capital would still be in Swordheart instead of here on the edge of the sea in Saltfast.

Had he tipped the scales the other way, the landscape would be rife with monsters, instead of mostly barren and growing over quickly with plants.

Someday, we'll have to cut the vines from cities and saw down the trees growing in fields. Someday, we'll have to make the roads smooth again and rebuild towers and churches and walls. Someday, we'll find the survivors in other lands beyond Cragspear and Ghregoiren, and establish trade routes once more.

Someday there will be new maps to make.

But for now, we cling here to the shore — this small band of survivors, the people of Cragspear and some we've drawn here from Ghregoiren, united under the rule of Stekkan the Merciful, King of Cragspear and Ghregoiren, Widower of Jendaya the First, who did not live out the first week of her rule.

He's married now to the daughter of Admiral Redtide and he reigns from Salt House, the Admiral's house on the sea. Some may call it a strange place to establish a government, but the sea is generous and the people are few. It's not so strange for their king to care more about their survival than his pomp — or at least it isn't for a king named for mercy.

And if this king is a little more taciturn and somber than the Stekkan Falrune people remember, well who can blame him after so much tragedy?

I like the name they've given him. It suits both this Stekkan and the Stekkan who came before.

And when the two of us find time to escape the work of ruling and the machinations of his council, we walk out along the shore and I try not to think of another sea I once knew or the soul that might yet sail it. Though perhaps — as in all my dearest hopes — he was drawn up by the Fisher King to the lands beyond where all is new and peace reigns.

It's a strange thing to look into my husband's deep

brown eyes, set in his lovely brown-skinned face. Even with the long white scar that bisects his forehead and cheek, he's still too beautiful by half. Too decorative. I look wrong beside him, just as his smile looks wrong in that devastating face, and his stalwart courage and stoic heroism wear this beauty like a grizzled veteran wears a flower crown. His voice though — his voice fits his temper perfectly, and when I close my eyes I see a different face.

He is king and I am merely his bride, and yet one would never think it, for he walks always in my shadow, watching every direction as if he is a great mastiff guarding his one perfect bone. I do not ask him to do otherwise. It comforts us both to walk that way and the people have grown used to the quiet peace of reclusive King Stekkan. His judgments are wise and when the whole of Saltfast must throw together to run a bucket brigade or free a ship caught on the sand, he is right there with the rest, carrying water or working an oar.

And if it seems strange that I have married a man whose proposal I turned down many times, it does not seem strange when our lips meet, and our fingers tangle, and we fall into our narrow, threadbare bed together. This part feels as though it's always been.

And in a few months' time when I bring his child into the world, I wonder if the babe will have his brown eyes, or possibly ... maybe ... the blue eyes I remember in my dreams.

"What do you dream of, my sun, my stars?" he whispers into my hair. His arms wrap around me from behind and the tide laps over our feet. I hear the happiness in his voice. It's a mirror to mine.

"I dream of mercy, Vargaard," I whisper and I thrill to speak the name I must guard for all our sakes. "And I dream of the Fisher King. But not for us — not yet."

"Not yet," he agrees as he kisses my temple. "Not yet, queen of my heart. Though I will defend you to the last drop of my blood."

And the duke was right. This was how it always had to be.

— THE END —

BEHIND THE SCENES

Writing is usually a lonely business but it really isn't that way for me. Besides the joy of two young boys who interrupt me diligently with observations about the world, I also have a wonderful friend and fellow author who reads all my scenes, helps me remember that I always feel this way when I reach this part of a story and it's nothing to worry about and basically tells me I'm a genius even though we both know it isn't true. Thank you for that, Melissa. Writing is more fun with you along for the ride.

I shouldn't neglect to thank my friend Eugenia, also, who offers her insights into all my books and also proofreads them. Without her reminding me, all my "lies" and "lays" would be wrong and you'd find a great many more typos. The cover for this book was done by the professionals at Polar Engine and they have my thanks for being easy to work with and creating lovely art for the cover. Thank you to the Noble Order of Female Fantasy Authors. Whenever I read about guilds in fantasy books, I want to be part of one and because of you, I am. It's great to have other people to work with and learn from and you are the best.

Thanks also to my beloved Cale who puts up with long rambling rants from me about writing and marketing books and has to listen to me analyze markets and algorithms he cares nothing about . You are a patient man And a HUGE THANK YOU to my patrons, **Mike Burgess, Jennifer Wood, Victoria Churchill** and **Carly Salsbury** for their support. You make my heart happy.

Visit Sarah's website for more information:
www.sarahklwilson.com